King Lear of the Steppes

Fabulous Novellas

King Lear of the Steppes

by
Ivan Turgenev

Translated from the Russian by
Constance Garnett

Skomlin
House of Memory

Skomlin
House of Memory and Imagination
For more information visit *www.skomlin.com*

A Skomlin Book
Melbourne, Australia

First published in 1870.
First English version, London 1906
© Skomlin, 2017

ISBN: 978-0-6482388-9-8 *(paperback)*
ISBN: 978-0-6482521-0-8 *eBook)*

 A catalogue record for this book is available from the National Library of Australia

The paper used in this publication meets the minimum requirements of ANSI/NISO Z39.48-1992 (R1997) (Permanence of Paper). The paper used in this book is from responsibly managed forests. Printed in the United States of America, the United Kingdom and Australia by Lightning Source, Inc.

KING LEAR OF THE STEPPES

We were a party of six, gathered together one winter evening at the house of an old college friend. The conversation turned on Shakespeare, on his types, and how profoundly and truly they were taken from the very heart of humanity. We admired particularly their truth to life, their actuality. Each of us spoke of the Hamlets, the Othellos, the Falstaffs, even the Richard the Thirds and Macbeths—the two last only potentially, it is true, resembling their prototypes—whom he had happened to come across.

'And I, gentlemen,' cried our host, a man well past middle age, 'used to know a King Lear!'

'How was that?' we questioned him.

'Oh, would you like me to tell you about him?'

'Please do.'

And our friend promptly began his narrative.

'All my childhood,' he began, 'and early youth, up to
the age of fifteen, I spent in the country, on the estate
of my mother, a wealthy landowner in X—— province.
Almost the most vivid impression, that has remained
in my memory of that far-off time, is the figure of our
nearest neighbour, Martin Petrovitch Harlov. Indeed it
would be difficult for such an impression to be oblite-
rated: I never in my life afterwards met anything in the
least like Harlov. Picture to yourselves a man of gigantic
stature. On his huge carcase was set, a little askew, and
without the least trace of a neck, a prodigious head.
A perfect haystack of tangled yellowish-grey hair stood
up all over it, growing almost down to the bushy eye-
brows. On the broad expanse of his purple face, that
looked as though it had been peeled, there protruded
a sturdy knobby nose; diminutive little blue eyes stared
out haughtily, and a mouth gaped open that was diminutive too, but crooked, chapped, and of the same colour
as the rest of the face. The voice that proceeded from
this mouth, though hoarse, was exceedingly strong and
resonant.... Its sound recalled the clank of iron bars,
carried in a cart over a badly paved road; and when
Harlov spoke, it was as though some one were shouting
in a high wind across a wide ravine. It was difficult to
tell just what Harlov's face expressed, it was such an
expanse.... One felt one could hardly take it all in at one
glance. But it was not disagreeable—a certain grandeur
indeed could be discerned in it, only it was exceedingly
astounding and unusual. And what hands he had—pos-
itive cushions! What fingers, what feet! I remember I
could never gaze without a certain respectful awe at the
four-foot span of Martin Petrovitch's back, at his shoulders, like millstones. But what especially struck me was
his ears! They were just like great twists of bread, full of

bends and curves; his cheeks seemed to support them on both sides. Martin Petrovitch used to wear—winter and summer alike—a Cossack dress of green cloth, girt about with a small Tcherkess strap, and tarred boots. I never saw a cravat on him; and indeed what could he have tied a cravat round? He breathed slowly and heavily, like a bull, but walked without a sound. One might have imagined that having got into a room, he was in constant fear of upsetting and overturning everything, and so moved cautiously from place to place, sideways for the most part, as though slinking by. He was possessed of a strength truly Herculean, and in consequence enjoyed great renown in the neighbourhood. Our common people retain to this day their reverence for Titanic heroes. Legends were invented about him. They used to recount that he had one day met a bear in the forest and had almost vanquished him; that having once caught a thief in his beehouse, he had flung him, horse and cart and all, over the hedge, and so on. Harlov himself never boasted of his strength. 'If my right hand is blessed,' he used to say, 'so it is God's will it should be!' He was proud, only he did not take pride in his strength, but in his rank, his descent, his common sense.

'Our family's descended from the Swede Harlus,' he used to maintain. 'In the princely reign of Ivan Vassilievitch the Dark (fancy how long ago!) he came to Russia, and that Swede Harlus did not wish to be a Finnish count—but he wished to be a Russian nobleman, and he was inscribed in the golden book. It's from him we Harlovs are sprung!... And by the same token, all of us Harlovs are born flaxen-haired, with light eyes and clean faces, because we're children of the snow!'

'But, Martin Petrovitch,' I once tried to object, 'there never was an Ivan Vassilievitch the Dark. Then was an Ivan Vassilievitch the Terrible. The Dark was the name given to the great prince Vassily Vassilievitch.'

'What nonsense will you talk next!' Harlov answered serenely; 'since I say so, so it was!'

One day my mother took it into her head to commend him to his face for his really remarkable incorruptibility.

'Ah, Natalia Nikolaevna!' he protested almost angrily; 'what a thing to praise me for, really! We gentlefolk can't be otherwise; so that no churl, no low-born, servile creature dare even imagine evil of us! I am a Harlov, my family has come down from'—here he pointed up somewhere very high aloft in the ceiling—'and me not be honest! How is it possible?'

Another time a high official, who had come into the neighbourhood and was staying with my mother, fancied he could make fun of Martin Petrovitch. The latter had again referred to the Swede Harlus, who came to Russia....

'In the days of King Solomon?' the official interrupted.

'No, not of King Solomon, but of the great Prince Ivan Vassilievitch the Dark.'

'But I imagine,' the official pursued, 'that your family is much more ancient, and goes back to antediluvian days, when there were still mastodons and megatheriums about.'

These scientific names were absolutely meaningless to Martin Petrovitch; but he realised that the dignitary was laughing at him.

'May be so,' he boomed, 'our family is, no doubt, very ancient; in those days when my ancestor was in Moscow, they do say there was as great a fool as your excellency living there, and such fools are not seen twice in a thousand years.'

The high official was in a furious rage, while Harlov threw his head back, stuck out his chin, snorted and disappeared. Two days later, he came in again. My mother began reproaching him. 'It's a lesson for him, ma'am,' interposed Harlov, 'not to fly off without knowing what

he's about, to find out whom he has to deal with first. He's young yet, he must be taught.' The dignitary was almost of the same age as Harlov; but this Titan was in the habit of regarding every one as not fully grown up. He had the greatest confidence in himself and was afraid of absolutely no one. 'Can they do anything to me? Where on earth is the man that can?' he would ask, and suddenly he would go off into a short but deafening guffaw.

My mother was exceedingly particular in her choice of acquaintances, but she made Harlov welcome with special cordiality and allowed him many privileges. Twenty-five years before, he had saved her life by holding up her carriage on the edge of a deep precipice, down which the horses had already fallen. The traces and straps of the harness broke, but Martin Petrovitch did not let go his hold of the wheel he had grasped, though the blood spurted out under his nails. My mother had arranged his marriage. She chose for his wife an orphan girl of seventeen, who had been brought up in her house; he was over forty at the time. Martin Petrovitch's wife was a frail creature—they said he carried her into his house in the palms of his hands—and she did not live long with him. She bore him two daughters, however. After her death, my mother continued her good offices to Martin Petrovitch. She placed his elder daughter in the district school, and afterwards found her a husband, and already had another in her eye for the second. Harlov was a fairly good manager. He had a little estate of nearly eight hundred acres, and had built on to his place a little, and the way the peasants obeyed him is indescribable. Owing to his stoutness, Harlov scarcely ever went anywhere on foot: the earth did not bear him. He used to go everywhere in a low racing droshky, himself driving a rawboned mare, thirty years old, with a scar on her shoulder, from a wound which she had received in the battle of Borodino, under the quartermaster of a cavalry regiment. This mare was always somehow lame in all four legs; she could not go at a walking pace, but could only change from a trot to a canter. She used to eat mugwort and wormwood along the hedges, which I have never noticed any other horse do. I remember I always used to wonder how such a broken-down nag

could draw such a fearful weight. I won't venture to repeat how many hundred-weight were attributed to our neighbour. In the droshky behind Martin Petrovitch's back perched his swarthy page, Maximka. With his face and whole person squeezed close up to his master, and his bare feet propped on the hind axle bar of the droshky, he looked like a little leaf or worm which had clung by chance to the gigantic carcase before him. This same page boy used once a week to shave Martin Petrovitch. He used, so they said, to stand on a table to perform this operation. Some jocose persons averred that he had to run round his master's chin. Harlov did not like staying long at home, and so one might often see him driving about in his invariable equipage, with the reins in one hand (the other he held smartly on his knee with the elbow crooked upwards), with a diminutive old cap on the very top of his head. He looked boldly about him with his little bear-like eyes, shouted in a voice of thunder to all the peasants, artisans, and tradespeople he met. Priests he greatly disliked, and he would send vigorous abjurations after them when he met them. One day on overtaking me (I was out for a stroll with my gun), he hallooed at a hare that lay near the road in such a way that I could not get the roar and ring of it out of my ears all day.

My mother, as I have already stated, made Martin Petrovitch very welcome. She knew what a profound respect
he entertained for her person. 'She is a real gentle-
woman, one of our sort,' was the way he used to refer to
her. He used to style her his benefactress, while she saw
in him a devoted giant, who would not have hesitated
to face a whole mob of peasants in defence of her; and
although no one foresaw the barest possibility of such a
contingency, still, to my mother's notions, in the absence
of a husband—she had early been left a widow—such a
champion as Martin Petrovitch was not to be despised.
And besides, he was a man of upright character, who
curried favour with no one, never borrowed money or
drank spirits; and no fool either, though he had received
no sort of education. My mother trusted Martin Petrovitch: when she took it into her head to make her
will, she asked him to witness it, and he drove home
expressly to fetch his round iron-rimmed spectacles,
without which he could not write. And with spectacles
on nose, he succeeded, in a quarter of an hour, with
many gasps and groans and great effort, in inscribing
his Christian name, father's name, and surname and his
rank and designation, tracing enormous quadrangular
letters, with tails and flourishes. Having completed this
task, he declared he was tired out, and that writing for
him was as hard work as catching fleas. Yes, my mother
had a respect for him... he was not, however, admitted beyond the dining-room in our house. He carried a
very strong odour about with him; there was a smell of
the earth, of decaying forest, of marsh mud about him.
'He's a forest-demon!' my old nurse would declare. At
dinner a special table used to be laid apart in a corner
for Martin Petrovitch, and he was not offended at that,
he knew other people were ill at ease sitting beside

him, and he too had greater freedom in eating. And he did eat too, as no one, I imagine, has eaten since the days of Polyphemus. At the very beginning of dinner, by way of a precautionary measure, they always served him a pot of some four pounds of porridge, 'else you'd eat me out of house and home,' my mother used to say. 'That I should, ma'am,' Martin Petrovitch would respond, grinning.

My mother liked to hear his reflections on any topic connected with the land. But she could not support the sound of his voice for long together. 'What's the meaning of it, my good sir!' she would exclaim; 'you might take something to cure yourself of it, really! You simply deafen me. Such a trumpet-blast!'

'Natalia Nikolaevna! benefactress!' Martin Petrovitch would rejoin, as a rule, 'I'm not responsible for my throat. And what medicine could have any effect on me—kindly tell me that? I'd better hold my tongue for a bit.'

In reality, I imagine, no medicine could have affected Martin Petrovitch. He was never ill.

He was not good at telling stories, and did not care for it. 'Much talking gives me asthma,' he used to remark reproachfully. It was only when one got him on to the year 1812—he had served in the militia, and had received a bronze medal, which he used to wear on festive occasions attached to a Vladimir ribbon—when one questioned him about the French, that he would relate some few anecdotes. He used, however, to maintain stoutly all the while that there never had been any Frenchmen, real ones, in Russia, only some poor marauders, who had straggled over from hunger, and that he had given many a good drubbing to such rabble in the forests.

IV

And yet even this self-confident, unflinching giant had his moments of melancholy and depression. Without any visible cause he would suddenly begin to be sad; he would lock himself up alone in his room, and hum— positively hum—like a whole hive of bees; or he would call his page Maximka, and tell him to read aloud to him out of the solitary book which had somehow found its way into his house, an odd volume of Novikovsky's *The Worker at Leisure*, or else to sing to him. And Maximka, who by some strange freak of chance, could spell out print, syllable by syllable, would set to work with the usual chopping up of the words and transference of the accent, bawling out phrases of the following description: 'but man in his wilfulness draws from this empty hypothesis, which he applies to the animal kingdom, utterly opposite conclusions. Every animal separately,' he says, 'is not capable of making me happy!' and so on. Or he would chant in a shrill little voice a mournful song, of which nothing could be distinguished but: 'Ee... eee... ee... a... ee... a... ee... Aaa... ska! O... oo... oo... bee... ee... ee... ee... la!'

While Martin Petrovitch would shake his head, make allusions to the mutability of life, how all things turn to ashes, fade away like grass, pass—and will return no more! A picture had somehow come into his hands, representing a burning candle, which the winds, with puffed-out cheeks, were blowing upon from all sides; below was the inscription: 'Such is the life of man.' He was very fond of this picture; he had hung it up in his own room, but at ordinary, not melancholy, times he used to keep it turned face to the wall, so that it might not depress him. Harlov, that colossus, was afraid of death! To the consolations of religion, to prayer, however, he rarely had recourse in his fits of melancholy.

Even then he chiefly relied on his own intelligence. He had no particular religious feeling; he was not often seen in church; he used to say, it is true, that he did not go on the ground that, owing to his corporeal dimensions, he was afraid of squeezing other people out. The fit of depression commonly ended in Martin Petrovitch's beginning to whistle, and suddenly, in a voice of thunder, ordering out his droshky, and dashing off about the neighbourhood, vigorously brandishing his disengaged hand over the peak of his cap, as though he would say, 'For all that, I don't care a straw!' He was a regular Russian.

V

Strong men, like Martin Petrovitch, are for the most part
of a phlegmatic disposition; but he, on the contrary, was
rather easily irritated. He was specially short-tempered
with a certain Bitchkov, who had found a refuge in our
house, where he occupied a position between that of a
buffoon and a dependant. He was the brother of Harlov's deceased wife, had been nicknamed Souvenir as
a little boy, and Souvenir he had remained for every
one, even the servants, who addressed him, it is true, as
Souvenir Timofeitch. His real name he seemed hardly to
know himself. He was a pitiful creature, looked down
upon by every one; a toady, in fact. He had no teeth
on one side of his mouth, which gave his little wrinkled face a crooked appearance. He was in a perpet-
ual fuss and fidget; he used to poke himself into the
maids' room, or into the counting-house, or into the
priest's quarters, or else into the bailiff's hut. He was
repelled from everywhere, but he only shrugged himself up, and screwed up his little eyes, and laughed a
pitiful mawkish laugh, like the sound of rinsing a bottle.
It always seemed to me that had Souvenir had money,
he would have turned into the basest person, unprin-
cipled, spiteful, even cruel. Poverty kept him within
bounds. He was only allowed drink on holidays. He
was decently dressed, by my mother's orders, since in
the evenings he took a hand in her game of picquet
or boston. Souvenir was constantly repeating, 'Certainly,
d'rectly, d'rectly.' 'D'rectly what?' my mother would ask,
with annoyance. He instantly drew back his hands, in
a scare, and lisped, 'At your service, ma'am!' Listening
at doors, backbiting, and, above all, quizzing, teasing,
were his sole interest, and he used to quiz as though
he had a right to, as though he were avenging himself
for something. He used to call Martin Petrovitch brother,

and tormented him beyond endurance. 'What made you kill my sister, Margarita Timofeevna?' he used to persist, wriggling about before him and sniggering. One day Martin Petrovitch was sitting in the billiard-room, a cool apartment, in which no one had ever seen a single fly, and which our neighbour, disliking heat and sunshine, greatly favoured on this account. He was sitting between the wall and the billiard-table. Souvenir was fidgeting before his bulky person, mocking him, grimacing.... Martin Petrovitch wanted to get rid of him, and thrust both hands out in front of him. Luckily for Souvenir he managed to get away, his brother-in-law's open hands came into collision with the edge of the billiard-table, and the billiard-board went flying off all its six screws.... What a mass of batter Souvenir would have been turned into under those mighty hands!

VI

I had long been curious to see how Martin Petrovitch arranged his household, what sort of a home he had. One day I invited myself to accompany him on horseback as far as Eskovo (that was the name of his estate). 'Upon my word, you want to have a look at my dominion,' was Martin Petrovitch's comment. 'By all means! I'll show you the garden, and the house, and the threshing-floor, and everything. I have plenty of everything.' We set off. It was reckoned hardly more than a couple of miles from our place to Eskovo. 'Here it is—my dominion!' Martin Petrovitch roared suddenly, trying to turn his immovable neck, and waving his arm to right and left. 'It's all mine!' Harlov's homestead lay on the top of a sloping hill. At the bottom, a few wretched-looking peasants' huts clustered close to a small pond. At the pond, on a washing platform, an old peasant woman in a check petticoat was beating some soaked linen with a bat.

'Axinia!' boomed Martin Petrovitch, but in such a note that the rooks flew up in a flock from an oat-field near.... 'Washing your husband's breeches?'

The peasant woman turned at once and bowed very low.

'Yes, sir,' sounded her weak voice.

'Ay, ay! Yonder, look,' Martin Petrovitch continued, proceeding at a trot alongside a half-rotting wattle fence, 'that is my hemp-patch; and that yonder's the peasants'; see the difference? And this here is my garden; the apple-trees I planted, and the willows I planted too. Else there was no timber of any sort here. Look at that, and learn a lesson!'

We turned into the courtyard, shut in by a fence; right

opposite the gate, rose an old tumbledown lodge, with a thatch roof, and steps up to it, raised on posts. On one side stood another, rather newer, and with a tiny attic; but it too was a ramshackly affair. 'Here you may learn a lesson again,' observed Harlov; 'see what a little manor-house our fathers lived in; but now see what a mansion I have built myself.' This 'mansion' was like a house of cards. Five or six dogs, one more ragged and hideous than another, welcomed us with barking. 'Sheepdogs!' observed Martin Petrovitch. 'Pure-bred Crimeans! Sh, damned brutes! I'll come and strangle you one after another!' On the steps of the new building, there came out a young man, in a long full nankeen overall, the husband of Martin Petrovitch's elder daughter. Skipping quickly up to the droshky, he respectfully supported his father-in-law under the elbow as he got up, and even made as though he would hold the gigantic feet, which the latter, bending his bulky person forward, lifted with a sweeping movement across the seat; then he assisted me to dismount from my horse.

'Anna!' cried Harlov, 'Natalia Nikolaevna's son has come to pay us a visit; you must find some good cheer for him. But where's Evlampia?' (Anna was the name of the elder daughter, Evlampia of the younger.)

'She's not at home; she's gone into the fields to get cornflowers,' responded Anna, appearing at a little window near the door.

'Is there any junket?' queried Harlov.

'Yes.'

'And cream too?'

'Yes.'

'Well, set them on the table, and I'll show the young gentleman my own room meanwhile. This way, please, this way,' he added, addressing me, and beckoning with his forefinger. In his own house he treated me less

21

familiarly; as a host he felt obliged to be more formally respectful. He led me along a corridor. 'Here is where I abide,' he observed, stepping sideways over the threshold of a wide doorway, 'this is my room. Pray walk in!'

His room turned out to be a big unplastered apartment, almost empty; on the walls, on nails driven in askew, hung two riding-whips, a three-cornered hat, reddish with wear, a single-barrelled gun, a sabre, a sort of curious horse-collar inlaid with metal plates, and the picture representing a burning candle blown on by the winds. In one corner stood a wooden settle covered with a particoloured rug. Hundreds of flies swarmed thickly about the ceiling; yet the room was cool. But there was a very strong smell of that peculiar odour of the forest which always accompanied Martin Petrovitch.

'Well, is it a nice room?' Harlov questioned me.

'Very nice.'

'Look-ye, there hangs my Dutch horse-collar,' Harlov went on, dropping into his familiar tone again. 'A splendid horse-collar! got it by barter off a Jew. Just you look at it!'

'It's a good horse-collar.'

'It's most practical. And just sniff it... what leather!' I smelt the horse-collar. It smelt of rancid oil and nothing else.

'Now, be seated,—there on the stool; make yourself at home,' observed Harlov, while he himself sank on to the settle, and seemed to fall into a doze, shutting his eyes and even beginning to snore. I gazed at him without speaking, with ever fresh wonder; he was a perfect mountain—there was no other word! Suddenly he started.

'Anna!' he shouted, while his huge stomach rose and fell like a wave on the sea; 'what are you about? Look sharp! Didn't you hear me?'

'Everything's ready, father; come in,' I heard his daughter's voice.

I inwardly marvelled at the rapidity with which Martin Petrovitch's behests had been carried out; and followed him into the drawing-room, where, on a table covered with a red cloth with white flowers on it, lunch was already prepared: junket, cream, wheaten bread, even powdered sugar and ginger. While I set to work on the junket, Martin Petrovitch growled affectionately, 'Eat, my friend, eat, my dear boy; don't despise our country cheer,' and sitting down again in a corner, again seemed to fall into a doze. Before me, perfectly motionless, with downcast eyes, stood Anna Martinovna, while I saw through the window her husband walking my cob up and down the yard, and rubbing the chain of the snaffle with his own hands.

VII

My mother did not like Harlov's elder daughter; she called her a stuck-up thing. Anna Martinovna scarcely ever came to pay us her respects, and behaved with chilly decorum in my mother's presence, though it was by her good offices she had been well educated at a boarding-school, and had been married, and on her wedding-day had received a thousand roubles and a yellow Turkish shawl, the latter, it is true, a trifle the worse for wear. She was a woman of medium height, thin, very brisk and rapid in her movements, with thick fair hair and a handsome dark face, on which the pale-blue narrow eyes showed up in a rather strange but pleasing way. She had a straight thin nose, her lips were thin too, and her chin was like the loop-end of a hair-pin. No one looking at her could fail to think: 'Well, you are a clever creature—and a spiteful one, too!' And for all that, there was something attractive about her too. Even the dark moles, scattered 'like buck-wheat' over her face, suited her and increased the feeling she inspired. Her hands thrust into her kerchief, she was slily watching me, looking downwards (I was seated, while she was standing). A wicked little smile strayed about her lips and her cheeks and in the shadow of her long eyelashes. 'Ugh, you pampered little fine gentleman!' this smile seemed to express. Every time she drew a breath, her nostrils slightly distended—this, too, was rather strange. But all the same, it seemed to me that were Anna Martinovna to love me, or even to care to kiss me with her thin cruel lips, I should simply bound up to the ceiling with delight. I knew she was very severe and exacting, that the peasant women and girls went in terror of her—but what of that? Anna Martinovna secretly excited my imagination... though after all, I was only fifteen then,—and at that age!...

Martin Petrovitch roused himself again, 'Anna!' he shouted, 'you ought to strum something on the piano-forte… young gentlemen are fond of that.'

I looked round; there was a pitiful semblance of a piano in the room.

'Yes, father,' responded Anna Martinovna. 'Only what am I to play the young gentleman? He won't find it interesting.'

'Why, what did they teach you at your young ladies' seminary?'

'I've forgotten everything—besides, the notes are broken.'

Anna Martinovna's voice was very pleasant, resonant and rather plaintive—like the note of some birds of prey.

'Very well,' said Martin Petrovitch, and he lapsed into dreaminess again. 'Well,' he began once more, 'wouldn't you like, then, to see the threshing-floor, and have a look round? Volodka will escort you.—Hi, Volodka!' he shouted to his son-in-law, who was still pacing up and down the yard with my horse, 'take the young gentleman to the threshing-floor… and show him my farming generally. But I must have a nap! So! good-bye!'

He went out and I after him. Anna Martinovna at once set to work rapidly, and, as it were, angrily, clearing the table. In the doorway, I turned and bowed to her. But she seemed not to notice my bow, and only smiled again, more maliciously than before.

I took my horse from Harlov's son-in-law and led him by the bridle. We went together to the threshing-floor, but as we discovered nothing very remarkable about it, and as he could not suppose any great interest in farming in a young lad like me, we returned through the garden to the main road.

VIII

I was well acquainted with Harlov's son-in-law. His name was Vladimir Vassilievitch Sletkin. He was an orphan, brought up by my mother, and the son of a petty official, to whom she had intrusted some business. He had first been placed in the district school, then he had entered the 'seignorial counting-house,' then he had been put into the service of the government stores, and, finally, married to the daughter of Martin Petrovitch. My mother used to call him a little Jew, and certainly, with his curly hair, his black eyes always moist, like damson jam, his hook nose, and wide red mouth, he did suggest the Jewish type. But the colour of his skin was white and he was altogether very good-looking. He was of a most obliging temper, so long as his personal advantage was not involved. Then he promptly lost all self-control from greediness, and was moved even to tears. He was ready to whine the whole day long to gain the paltriest trifle; he would remind one a hundred times over of a promise, and be hurt and complain if it were not carried out at once. He liked sauntering about the fields with a gun; and when he happened to get a hare or a wild duck, he would thrust his booty into his game-bag with peculiar zest, saying, 'Now, you may be as tricky as you like, you won't escape me! Now you're *mine!*'

'You've a good horse,' he began in his lisping voice, as he assisted me to get into the saddle; 'I ought to have a horse like that! But where can I get one? I've no such luck. If you'd ask your mamma, now—remind her.'

'Why, has she promised you one?'

'Promised? No; but I thought that in her great kind-ness——'

'You should apply to Martin Petrovitch.'

'To Martin Petrovitch?' Sletkin repeated, dwelling on each syllable. 'To him I'm no better than a worthless page, like Maximka. He keeps a tight hand on us, that he does, and you get nothing from him for all your toil.'

'Really?'

'Yes, by God. He'll say, "My word's sacred!"—and there, it's as though he's chopped it off with an axe. You may beg or not, it's all one. Besides, Anna Martinovna, my wife, is not in such favour with him as Evlampia Martinovna. O merciful God, bless us and save us!' he suddenly interrupted himself, flinging up his hands in despair. 'Look! what's that? A whole half-rood of oats, our oats, some wretch has gone and cut. The villain! Just see! Thieves! thieves! It's a true saying, to be sure, don't trust Eskovo, Beskovo, Erino, and Byelino! (these were the names of four villages near). Ah, ah, what a thing! A rouble and a half's worth, or, maybe, two roubles' loss!'

In Sletkin's voice, one could almost hear sobs. I gave my horse a poke in the ribs and rode away from him.

Sletkin's ejaculations still reached my hearing, when suddenly at a turn in the road, I came upon the second daughter of Harlov, Evlampia, who had, in the words of Anna Martinovna, gone into the fields to get cornflowers. A thick wreath of those flowers was twined about her head. We exchanged bows in silence. Evlampia, too, was very good-looking; as much so as her sister, though in a different style. She was tall and stoutly built; everything about her was on a large scale: her head, and her feet and hands, and her snow-white teeth, and especially her eyes, prominent, languishing eyes, of the dark blue of glass beads. Everything about her, while still beautiful, had positively a monumental character (she was a true daughter of Martin Petrovitch). She did not, it seemed, know what to do with her massive fair mane, and she had twisted it in three plaits round her head. Her mouth was charming, crimson and fresh as a rose, and as she talked her upper lip was lifted in the middle in a very fascinating way. But there was something wild and almost fierce in the glance of her huge eyes. 'A free bird, wild Cossack breed,' so Martin Petrovitch used to speak of her. I was in awe of her.... This stately beauty reminded one of her father.

I rode on a little farther and heard her singing in a strong, even, rather harsh voice, a regular peasant voice; suddenly she ceased. I looked round and from the crest of the hill saw her standing beside Harlov's son-in-law, facing the rood of oats. The latter was gesticulating and pointing, but she stood without stirring. The sun lighted up her tall figure, and the wreath of cornflowers shone brilliantly blue on her head.

IX

I believe I have already mentioned that, for this second daughter of Harlov's too, my mother had already prepared a match. This was one of the poorest of our neighbours, a retired army major, Gavrila Fedulitch Zhitkov, a man no longer young, and, as he himself expressed it, not without a certain complacency, however, as though recommending himself, 'battered and broken down.' He could barely read and write, and was exceedingly stupid but secretly aspired to become my mother's steward, as he felt himself to be a 'man of action.' 'I can warm the peasant's hides for them, if I can do anything,' he used to say, almost gnashing his own teeth, 'because I was used to it,' he used to explain, 'in my former duties, I mean.' Had Zhitkov been less of a fool, he would have realised that he had not the slightest chance of being steward to my mother, seeing that, for that, it would have been necessary to get rid of the present steward, one Kvitsinsky, a very capable Pole of great character, in whom my mother had the fullest confidence. Zhitkov had a long face, like a horse's; it was all overgrown with hair of a dusty whitish colour; his cheeks were covered with it right up to the eyes; and even in the severest frosts, it was sprinkled with an abundant sweat, like drops of dew. At the sight of my mother, he drew himself upright as a post, his head positively quivered with zeal, his huge hands slapped a little against his thighs, and his whole person seemed to express: 'Command!... and I will strive my utmost!' My mother was under no illusion on the score of his abilities, which did not, however, hinder her from taking steps to marry him to Evlampia.

'Only, will you be able to manage her, my good sir?' she asked him one day.

Zhitkov smiled complacently.

'Upon my word, Natalia Nikolaevna! I used to keep a whole regiment in order; they were tame enough in my hands; and what's this? A trumpery business!'

'A regiment's one thing, sir, but a well-bred girl, a wife, is a very different matter,' my mother observed with displeasure.

'Upon my word, ma'am! Natalia Nikolaevna!' Zhitkov cried again, 'that we're quite able to understand. In one word: a young lady, a delicate person!'

'Well!' my mother decided at length, 'Evlampia won't let herself be trampled upon.'

X

One day—it was the month of June, and evening was coming on—a servant announced the arrival of Martin Petrovitch. My mother was surprised: we had not seen him for over a week, but he had never visited us so late before. 'Something has happened!' she exclaimed in an undertone. The face of Martin Petrovitch, when he rolled into the room and at once sank into a chair near the door, wore such an unusual expression, it was so preoccupied and positively pale, that my mother involuntarily repeated her exclamation aloud. Martin Petrovitch fixed his little eyes upon her, was silent for a space, sighed heavily, was silent again, and articulated at last that he had come about something... which... was of a kind, that on account of....

Muttering these disconnected words, he suddenly got up and went out.

My mother rang, ordered the footman, who appeared, to overtake Martin Petrovitch at once and bring him back without fail, but the latter had already had time to get into his droshky and drive away.

Next morning my mother, who was astonished and even alarmed, as much by Martin Petrovitch's strange behaviour as by the extraordinary expression of his face, was on the point of sending a special messenger to him, when he made his appearance. This time he seemed more composed.

'Tell me, my good friend, tell me,' cried my mother, directly she saw him, 'what ever has happened to you? I thought yesterday, upon my word I did.... "Mercy on us!" I thought, "Hasn't our old friend gone right off his head?"'

'I've not gone off my head, madam,' answered Martin

Petrovitch; 'I'm not that sort of man. But I want to consult with you.'

'What about?'

'I'm only in doubt, whether it will be agreeable to you in this same contingency——'

'Speak away, speak away, my good sir, but more simply. Don't alarm me! What's this same contingency? Speak more plainly. Or is it your melancholy come upon you again?'

Harlov scowled. 'No, it's not melancholy—that comes upon me in the new moon; but allow me to ask you, madam, what do you think about death?'

My mother was taken aback. 'About what?'

'About death. Can death spare any one whatever in this world?'

'What have you got in your head, my good friend? Who of us is immortal? For all you're born a giant, even to you there'll be an end in time.'

'There will! oh, there will!' Harlov assented and he looked downcast. 'I've had a vision come to me in my dreams,' he brought out at last.

'What are you saying?' my mother interrupted him.

'A vision in my dreams,' he repeated—'I'm a seer of visions, you know!'

'You!'

'I. Didn't you know it?' Harlov sighed. 'Well, so.... Over a week ago, madam, I lay down, on the very last day of eating meat before St. Peter's fast-day; I lay down after dinner to rest a bit, well, and so I fell asleep, and dreamed a raven colt ran into the room to me. And this colt began sporting about and grinning. Black as a beetle was the raven colt.' Harlov ceased.

'Well?' said my mother.

'And all of a sudden this same colt turns round, and gives me a kick in the left elbow, right in the funny bone.... I waked up; my arm would not move nor my leg either. Well, thinks I, it's paralysis; however, I worked them up and down, and got them to move again; only there were shooting pains in the joints a long time, and there are still. When I open my hand, the pains shoot through the joints.'

'Why, Martin Petrovitch, you must have lain upon your arm somehow and crushed it.'

'No, madam; pray, don't talk like that! It was an intimation... referring to my death, I mean.'

'Well, upon my word,' my mother was beginning.

'An intimation. Prepare thyself, man, as 'twere to say. And therefore, madam, here is what I have to announce to you, without a moment's delay. Not wishing,' Harlov suddenly began shouting, 'that the same death should come upon me, the servant of God, unawares, I have planned in my own mind this: to divide—now during my lifetime—my estate between my two daughters, Anna and Evlampia, according as God Almighty directs me—' Martin Petrovitch stopped, groaned, and added, 'without a moment's delay.'

'Well, that would be a good idea,' observed my mother; 'though I think you have no need to be in a hurry.'

'And seeing that herein I desire,' Harlov continued, raising his voice still higher, 'to be observant of all due order and legality, so I humbly beg your young son, Dmitri Semyonovitch—I would not venture, madam, to trouble you—I beg the said Dmitri Semyonovitch, your son, and I claim of my kinsman, Bitchkov, as a plain duty, to assist at the ratification of the formal act and transference of possession to my two daughters— Anna, married, and Evlampia, spinster. Which act will be drawn up in readiness the day after tomorrow at twelve o'clock, at my own place, Eskovo, also called Kozulkino, in the presence of the ruling authorities and functionaries, who are thereto invited.'

Martin Petrovitch with difficulty reached the end of this speech, which he had obviously learnt by heart, and which was interspersed with frequent sighs.... He seemed to have no breath left in his chest; his pale face was crimson again, and he several times wiped the sweat off it.

'So you've already composed the deed dividing your property?' my mother queried. 'When did you manage that?'

'I managed it... oh! Neither eating, nor drinking——'

'Did you write it yourself?'

'Volodka... oh! helped.'

'And have you forwarded a petition?'

'I have, and the chamber has sanctioned it, and notice has been given to the district court, and the temporary division of the local court has... oh!... been notified to be present.'

My mother laughed. 'I see, Martin Petrovitch, you've made every arrangement already—and how quickly. You've not spared money, I should say?'

'No, indeed, madam.'

'Well, well. And you say you want to consult with me. Well, my little Dmitri can go; and I'll send Souvenir with him, and speak to Kvitsinsky.... But you haven't invited Gavrila Fedulitch?'

'Gavrila Fedulitch—Mr. Zhitkov—has had notice... from me also. As a betrothed, it was only fitting.'

Martin Petrovitch had obviously exhausted all the

resources of his eloquence. Besides, it always seemed to me that he did not look altogether favourably on the match my mother had made for his daughter; possibly, he had expected a more advantageous marriage for his darling Evlampia.

He got up from his chair, and made a scrape with his foot. 'Thank you for your consent.'

'Where are you off to?' asked my mother. 'Stay a bit; I'll order some lunch to be served you.'

'Much obliged,' responded Harlov. 'But I cannot.... Oh! I must get home.'

He backed and was about to move sideways, as his habit was, through the door.

'Stop, stop a minute,' my mother went on, 'can you possibly mean to make over the whole of your property without reserve to your daughters?'

'Certainly, without reserve.'

'Well, but how about yourself—where are you going to live?'

Harlov positively flung up his hands in amazement. 'You ask where? In my house, at home, as I've lived hitherto... so henceforward. Whatever difference could there be?'

'You have such confidence in your daughters and your son-in-law, then?'

'Were you pleased to speak of Volodka? A poor stick like him? Why, I can do as I like with him, whatever it is... what authority has he? As for them, my daughters, that is, to care for me till I'm in the grave, to give me meat and drink, and clothe me.... Merciful heavens! it's their first duty. I shall not long be an eyesore to them. Death's not over the hills—it's upon my shoulders.'

'Death is in God's hands,' observed my mother;

'though that is their duty, to be sure. Only pardon me, Martin Petrovitch; your elder girl, Anna, is well known to be proud and imperious, and—well—the second has a fierce look....'

'Natalia Nikolaevna!' Harlov broke in, 'why do you say that?... Why, as though they... My daughters... Why, as though I... Forget their duty? Never in their wildest dreams.... Offer opposition? To whom? Their parent... Dare to do such a thing? Have they not my curse to fear? They've passed their life long in fear and in submission—and all of a sudden... Good Lord!'

Harlov choked, there was a rattle in his throat.

'Very well, very well,' my mother made haste to soothe him; 'only I don't understand all the same what has put it into your head to divide the property up now. It would have come to them afterwards, in any case. I imagine it's your melancholy that's at the bottom of it all.'

'Eh, ma'am,' Harlov rejoined, not without vexation, 'you will keep coming back to that. There is, maybe, a higher power at work in this, and you talk of melancholy. I thought to do this, madam, because in my own person, while still in life, I wish to decide in my presence, who is to possess what, and with what I will reward each, so that they may possess, and feel thankfulness, and carry out my wishes, and what their father and benefactor has resolved upon, they may accept as a bountiful gift.'

Harlov's voice broke again.

'Come, that's enough, that's enough, my good friend,' my mother cut him short; 'or your raven colt will be putting in an appearance in earnest.'

'O Natalia Nikolaevna, don't talk to me of it,' groaned Harlov. 'That's my death come after me. Forgive my intrusion. And you, my little sir, I shall have the honour of expecting you the day after tomorrow.'

Martin Petrovitch went out; my mother looked after him, and shook her head significantly. 'This is a bad business,' she murmured, 'a bad business. You noticed'—she addressed herself to me—'he talked, and all the while seemed blinking, as though the sun were in his eyes; that's a bad sign. When a man's like that, his heart's sure to be heavy, and misfortune threatens him. You must go over the day after tomorrow with Vikenty Osipovitch and Souvenir.'

On the day appointed, our big family coach, with seats for four, harnessed with six bay horses, and with the head coachman, the grey-bearded and portly Alexeitch, on the box, rolled smoothly up to the steps of our house. The importance of the act upon which Harlov was about to enter, and the solemnity with which he had invited us, had had their effect on my mother. She had herself given orders for this extraordinary state equipage to be brought out, and had directed Souvenir and me to put on our best clothes. She obviously wished to show respect to her protégé. As for Kvitsinsky, he always wore a frock-coat and white tie. Souvenir chattered like a magpie all the way, giggled, wondered whether his brother would apportion him anything, and thereupon called him a dummy and an old fogey. Kvitsinsky, a man of severe and bilious temperament, could not put up with it at last 'What can induce you,' he observed, in his distinct Polish accent, 'to keep up such a continual unseemly chatter? Can you really be incapable of sitting quiet without these "wholly superfluous" (his favourite phrase) inanities?' 'All right, d'rectly,' Souvenir muttered discontentedly, and he fixed his squinting eyes on the carriage window. A quarter of an hour had not passed, the smoothly trotting horses had scarcely begun to get warm under the straps of their new harness, when Harlov's homestead came into sight. Through the widely open gate, our coach rolled into the yard. The diminutive postillion, whose legs hardly reached half-way down his horses' body, for the last time leaped up with a babyish shriek into the soft saddle, old Alexeitch at once spread out and raised his elbows, a slight 'wo-o' was heard, and we stopped. The dogs did not bark to greet us, and the serf boys, in long smocks that gaped open over their big stomachs, had all hidden themselves. Harlov's son-in-law was awaiting us in the doorway. I remember I was particularly struck by the birch boughs stuck in on both sides of the steps, as though it were Trinity Sunday. 'Grandeur upon grandeur,' Souvenir, who was the first to alight, squeaked through his nose. And certainly there was a solemn air about everything. Harlov's son-in-law was wearing a plush cravat with a satin bow, and an extraordinarily tight tail-coat; while Maximka, who popped out behind his back, had his hair so saturated with kvas, that it positively dripped. We went into the parlour, and saw Martin Petrovitch towering— yes, positively towering—motionless, in the middle of the room. I don't know what Souvenir's and Kvitsinsky's feelings were at the sight of his colossal figure; but I felt something akin to awe. Martin Petrovitch was attired in a grey Cossack coat—his militia uniform of 1812 it must have been—with a black stand-up collar. A bronze medal was to be seen on his breast, a sabre hung at his side; he laid his left hand on the hilt, with his right he was leaning on the table, which was covered with a red cloth. Two sheets of paper, full of writing, lay on the table. Harlov stood motionless, not even gasping; and what dignity was expressed in his attitude, what confidence in himself, in his unlimited and unquestionable power! He barely greeted us with a motion of the head, and barely articulating 'Be seated!' pointed the forefinger of his left hand in the direction of some chairs set in a row. Against the right-hand wall of the parlour were standing Harlov's daughters wearing their Sunday clothes: Anna, in a shot lilac-green dress, with a yellow silk sash; Evlampia, in pink, with crimson ribbons. Near them stood Zhitkov, in a new uniform, with the habitual expression of dull and greedy expectation in his eyes, and with a greater profusion of sweat than usual over his hirsute countenance. On the left side of the room sat the priest, in a threadbare snuff-coloured cassock, an old man, with rough brown hair. This head of hair, and the dejected lack-lustre eyes, and the big wrinkled hands, which seemed a burden even to himself, and lay like two rocks on his knees, and the tarred boots which peeped out beneath his cassock, all seemed to tell of a joyless laborious life. His parish was a very poor one. Beside him was the local police captain, a fattish, palish, dirty-looking little gentleman, with soft puffy little hands and feet, black eyes, black short-clipped moustaches, a continual cheerful but yet sickly little smile on his face. He had the reputation of being a great taker of bribes, and even a tyrant, as the expression was in those days. But not only the gentry, even the peasants were used to him, and liked him. He bent very free and easy and rather ironical looks around him; it was clear that all this 'procedure' amused him. In reality, the only part that had any interest for him was the light lunch and spirits in store for us. But the attorney sitting near him, a lean man with a long face, narrow whiskers from his ears to his nose, as they were worn in the days of Alexander the First, was absorbed with his whole soul in Martin Petrovitch's proceedings, and never took his big serious eyes off him. In his concentrated attention and sympathy, he kept moving and twisting his lips, though without opening his mouth. Souvenir stationed himself next him, and began talking to him in a whisper, after first informing me that he was the chief freemason in the province. The temporary division of the local court consists, as every one knows, of the police captain, the attorney, and the rural police commissioner; but the latter was either absent or kept himself in the background, so that I did not notice him. He bore, however, the nickname 'the non-existent' among us in the district, just as there are tramps called 'the non-identified.' I sat next Souvenir, Kvitsinsky next me. The face of the practical Pole showed unmistakeable annoyance at our 'wholly superfluous' expedition, and unnecessary waste of time.... 'A grand lady's caprices! these Russian grandees' fancies!' he seemed to be murmuring to himself.... 'Ugh, these Russians!'

When we were all seated, Martin Petrovitch hunched his shoulders, cleared his throat, scanned us all with his bear-like little eyes, and with a noisy sigh began as follows:

'Gentlemen, I have called you together for the following purpose. I am grown old, gentlemen, and overcome by infirmities.... Already I have had an intimation, the hour of death steals on, like a thief in the night.... Isn't that so, father?' he addressed the priest.

The priest started. 'Quite so, quite so,' he mumbled, his beard shaking.

'And therefore,' continued Martin Petrovitch, suddenly raising his voice, 'not wishing the said death to come upon me unawares, I purposed ...' Martin Petrovitch proceeded to repeat, word for word, the speech he had made to my mother two days before. 'In accordance with this my determination,' he shouted louder than ever, 'this deed' (he struck his hand on the papers lying on the table) 'has been drawn up by me, and the presiding authorities have been invited by me, and wherein my will consists the following points will treat. I have ruled, my day is over!'

Martin Petrovitch put his round iron spectacles on his nose, took one of the written sheets from the table, and began:

'Deed of partition of the estate of the retired non-commissioned officer and nobleman, Martin Harlov, drawn up by himself in his full and right understanding, and by his own good judgment, and wherein is precisely defined what benefits are assigned to his two daughters, Anna and Evlampia—bow!'—(they bowed), 'and in what way the serfs and other property, and live stock, be apportioned between the said daughters! Under my hand!'

'This is their document!' the police captain whispered to Kvitsinsky, with his invariable smile, 'they want to read it for the beauty of the style, but the legal deed is made out formally, without all these flourishes.'

Souvenir was beginning to snigger....

'In accordance with my will,' put in Harlov, who had caught the police captain's remark.

'In accordance in every point,' the latter hastened to respond cheerfully; 'only, as you're aware, Martin Petrovitch, there's no dispensing with formality. And unnecessary details have been removed. For the chamber can't enter into the question of spotted cows and fancy drakes.'

'Come here!' boomed Harlov to his son-in-law, who had come into the room behind us, and remained standing with an obsequious air near the door. He skipped up to his father-in-law at once.

'There, take it and read! It's hard for me. Only mind and don't mumble it! Let all the gentlemen present be able to understand it.'

Sletkin took the paper in both hands, and began timidly, but distinctly, and with taste and feeling, to read the deed of partition. There was set forth in it with the greatest accuracy just what was assigned to Anna and what to Evlampia, and how the division was to be made. Harlov from time to time interspersed the reading with phrases. 'Do you hear, that's for you, Anna, for your zeal!' or, 'That I give you, Evlampia!' and both the sisters bowed, Anna from the waist, Evlampia simply with a motion of the head. Harlov looked at them with stern dignity. 'The farm house' (the little new building) was assigned by him to Evlampia, as the younger daughter, 'by the well-known custom.' The reader's voice quivered and resounded at these words, unfavourable for himself; while Zhitkov licked his lips. Evlampia gave him a side-long glance; had I been in Zhitkov's shoes, I should not have liked that glance. The scornful expression, charac-teristic of Evlampia, as of every genuine Russian beauty, had a peculiar shade at that moment. For himself, Martin Petrovitch reserved the right to go on living in the rooms he occupied, and assigned to himself, under the name of 'rations,' a full allowance 'of normal provisions,' and ten roubles a month for clothes. The last phrase of the deed Harlov wished to read himself. 'And this my paren-tal will,' it ran, 'to carry out and observe is a sacred and binding duty on my daughters, seeing it is a command; seeing that I am, after God, their father and head, and am not bounden to render an account to any, nor have so rendered. And do they carry out my will, so will my fatherly blessing be with them, but should they not so do, which God forbid, then will they be overtaken by my paternal curse that cannot be averted, now and for ever, amen!' Harlov raised the deed high above his head. Anna at once dropped on her knees and touched the ground with her forehead; her husband, too, doubled up after her. 'Well, and you?' Harlov turned to Evlampia. She crimsoned all over, and she too bowed to the earth; Zhitkov bent his whole carcase forward.

'Sign!' cried Harlov, pointing his forefinger to the bottom of the deed. 'Here: "I thank and accept, Anna. I thank and accept, Evlampia!"'

Both daughters rose, and signed one after another. Sletkin rose too, and was feeling after the pen, but Harlov moved him aside, sticking his middle finger into his cravat, so that he gasped. The silence lasted a moment. Suddenly Martin Petrovitch gave a sort of sob, and muttering, 'Well, now it's all yours!' moved away. His daughters and son-in-law looked at one another, went up to him and began kissing him just above his elbow. His shoulder they could not reach.

The police captain read the real formal document, the deed of gift, drawn up by Martin Petrovitch. Then he went out on to the steps with the attorney and explained what had taken place to the crowd assembled at the gates, consisting of the witnesses required by law and other people from the neighbourhood, Harlov's peasants, and a few house-serfs. Then began the ceremony of the new owners entering into possession. They came out, too, upon the steps, and the police captain pointed to them when, slightly scowling with one eyebrow, while his careless face assumed for an instant a threatening air, he exhorted the crowd to 'subordination.' He might well have dispensed with these exhortations: a less unruly set of countenances than those of the Harlov peasants, I imagine, have never existed in creation. Clothed in thin smocks and torn sheepskins, but very tightly girt round their waists, as is always the peasants' way on solemn occasions, they stood motionless as though cut out of stone, and whenever the police captain uttered any exclamation such as, 'D'ye hear, you brutes? d'ye understand, you devils?' they suddenly bowed all at once, as though at the word of command. Each of these 'brutes and devils' held his cap tight in both hands, and never took his eyes off the window, where Martin Petrovitch's figure was visible. The witnesses themselves were hardly less awed. 'Is any impediment known to you,' the police captain roared at them, 'against the entrance into possession of these the sole and legitimate heirs and daughters of Martin Petrovitch Harlov?'

All the witnesses seemed to huddle together at once.

'Do you know any, you devils?' the police captain shouted again.

'We know nothing, your excellency,' responded sturdily a little old man, marked with small-pox, with a clipped beard and whiskers, an old soldier.

'I say! Eremeitch's a bold fellow!' the witnesses said of him as they dispersed.

In spite of the police captain's entreaties, Harlov would not come out with his daughters on to the steps. 'My subjects will obey my will without that!' he answered. Something like sadness had come over him on the completion of the conveyance. His face had grown pale. This new unprecedented expression of sadness looked so out of place on Martin Petrovitch's broad and kindly features that I positively was at a loss what to think. Was an attack of melancholy coming over him? The peasants, on their side, too, were obviously puzzled. And no wonder! 'The master's alive,—there he stands, and such a master, too; Martin Petrovitch! And all of a sudden he won't be their owner.... A queer thing!' I don't know whether Harlov had an inkling of the notions that were straying through his 'subjects' heads, or whether he wanted to display his power for the last time, but he suddenly opened the little window, stuck his head out, and shouted in a voice of thunder, 'obedience!' Then he slammed-to the window. The peasants' bewilderment was certainly not dispelled nor decreased by this proceeding. They became stonier than ever, and even seemed to cease looking at anything. The group of house-serfs (among them were two sturdy wenches, in short chintz gowns, with muscles such as one might perhaps match in Michael Angelo's 'Last Judgment,' and one utterly decrepit old man, hoary with age and half blind, in a threadbare frieze cloak, rumoured to have been 'cornet-player' in the days of Potemkin,—the page Maximka, Harlov had reserved for himself) this group showed more life than the peasants; at least, it moved restlessly about. The new mistresses themselves were very dignified in their attitude, especially Anna. Her thin lips tightly compressed, she looked obstinately down...

her stern figure augured little good to the house-serfs. Evlampia, too, did not raise her eyes; only once she turned round and deliberately, as it were with surprise, scanned her betrothed, Zhitkov, who had thought fit, following Sletkin, to come out, too, on to the steps. 'What business have you here?' those handsome prominent eyes seemed to demand. Sletkin was the most changed of all. A bustling cheeriness showed itself in his whole bearing, as though he were overtaken by hunger; the movements of his head and his legs were as obsequious as ever, but how gleefully he kept working his arms, how fussily he twitched his shoulder-blades. 'Arrived at last!' he seemed to say. Having finished the ceremony of the entrance into possession, the police captain, whose mouth was literally watering at the prospect of lunch, rubbed his hands in that peculiar manner which usually precedes the tossing-off of the first glass of spirits. But it appeared that Martin Petrovitch wished first to have a service performed with sprinklings of holy water. The priest put on an ancient and decrepit chasuble; a decrepit deacon came out of the kitchen, with difficulty kindling the incense in an old brazen church-vessel. The service began. Harlov sighed continually; he was unable, owing to his corpulence, to bow to the ground, but crossing himself with his right hand and bending his head, he pointed with the forefinger of his left hand to the floor. Sletkin positively beamed and even shed tears. Zhitkov, with dignity, in martial fashion, flourished his fingers only slightly between the third and fourth button of his uniform. Kvitsinsky, as a Catholic, remained in the next room. But the attorney prayed so fervently, sighed so sympathetically after Martin Petrovitch, and so persistently muttered and chewed his lips, turning his eyes upwards, that I felt moved, as I looked at him, and began to pray fervently too. At the conclusion of the service and the sprinkling with holy water, during which every one present, even the blind cornet-player, the contemporary of Potemkin, even Kvitsinsky, moistened their eyes with holy water, Anna and Evlampia once more, at Martin Petrovitch's bidding, prostrated themselves to the ground to thank him. Then at last came the moment of lunch. There were a great many dishes and all very nice; we all ate terribly much. The inevitable bottle of Don wine made its appearance. The police captain, who was of all of us the most familiar with the usages of the world, and besides, the representative of government, was the first to propose the toast to the health 'of the fair proprietresses!' Then he proposed we should drink to the health of our most honoured and most generous-hearted friend, Martin Petrovitch. At the words 'most generous-hearted,' Sletkin uttered a shrill little cry and ran to kiss his benefactor.... 'There, that'll do, that'll do,' muttered Harlov, as it were with annoyance, keeping him off with his elbow.... But at this point a not quite pleasant, as they say, incident took place.

XIV

Souvenir, who had been drinking continuously ever since the beginning of luncheon, suddenly got up from his chair as red as a beetroot, and pointing his finger at Martin Petrovitch, went off into his mawkish, paltry laugh.

'Generous-hearted! Generous-hearted!' he began croaking; 'but we shall see whether this generosity will be much to his taste when he's stripped naked, the servant of God... and out in the snow, too!'

'What rot are you talking, fool?' said Harlov contemptuously.

'Fool! fool!' repeated Souvenir. 'God Almighty alone knows which of us is the real fool. But you, brother, did my sister, your wife, to her death, and now you've done for yourself... ha-ha-ha!'

'How dare you insult our honoured benefactor?' Sletkin began shrilly, and, tearing himself away from Martin Petrovitch, whose shoulder he had clutched, he flew at Souvenir. 'But let me tell you, if our benefactor desires it, we can cancel the deed this very minute!'

'And yet, you'll strip him naked, and turn him out into the snow ...' returned Souvenir, retreating behind Kvitsinsky.

'Silence!' thundered Harlov. 'I'll pound you into a jelly! And you hold your tongue too, puppy!' he turned to Sletkin; 'don't put in your word where you're not wanted! If I, Martin Petrovitch Harlov, have decided to make a deed of partition, who can cancel the same act against my will? Why, in the whole world there is no power....'

'Martin Petrovitch!' the attorney began in a mellow bass—he too had drunk a good deal, but his dignity was only increased thereby—'but how if the gentleman has spoken the truth? You have done a generous action; to be sure, but how if—God forbid—in reality in place of fitting gratitude, some affront come of it?'

I stole a glance at both Martin Petrovitch's daughters. Anna's eyes were simply pinned upon the speaker, and a face more spiteful, more snake-like, and more beautiful in its very spite I had certainly never seen! Evlampia sat turned away, with her arms folded. A smile more scornful than ever curved her full, rosy lips.

Harlov got up from his chair, opened his mouth, but apparently his tongue failed him.... He suddenly brought his fist down on the table, so that everything in the room danced and rang.

'Father,' Anna said hurriedly, 'they do not know us, and that is why they judge of us so. But don't, please, make yourself ill. You are angered for nothing, indeed; see, your face is, as it were, twisted awry.'

Harlov looked towards Evlampia; she did not stir, though Zhitkov, sitting beside her, gave her a poke in the side.

'Thank you, my daughter Anna,' said Harlov huskily; 'you are a sensible girl; I rely upon you and on your husband too.' Sletkin once more gave vent to a shrill little sound; Zhitkov expanded his chest and gave a little scrape with his foot; but Harlov did not observe his efforts. 'This dolt,' he went on, with a motion of his chin in the direction of Souvenir, 'is pleased to get a chance to teaze me; but you, my dear sir,' he addressed himself to the attorney, 'it is not for you to pass judgment on Martin Harlov; that is something beyond you. Though you are a man in official position, your words are most foolish. Besides, the deed is done, there will be no going back from my determination.... Now, I will wish you good-day, I am going away. I am no longer the master of this house, but a guest in it. Anna, do you do your best; but I will go to my own room. Enough!'

Martin Petrovitch turned his back on us, and, without adding another word, walked deliberately out of the room.

This sudden withdrawal on the part of our host could not but break up the party, especially as the two hostesses also vanished not long after. Sletkin vainly tried to keep us. The police captain did not fail to blame the attorney for his uncalled-for candour. 'Couldn't help it!' the latter responded.... 'My conscience spoke.'

'There, you see that he's a mason,' Souvenir whispered to me.

'Conscience!' retorted the police captain. 'We know all about your conscience! I suppose it's in your pocket, just the same as it is with us sinners!'

The priest, meanwhile, even though already on his feet, foreseeing the speedy termination of the repast, lifted mouthful after mouthful to his mouth without a pause.

'You've got a fine appetite, I see,' Sletkin observed to him sharply.

'Storing up for the future,' the priest responded with a meek grimace; years of hunger were expressed in that reply.

The carriages rattled up... and we separated. On the way home, no one hindered Souvenir's chatter and silly tricks, as Kvitsinsky had announced that he was sick of all this 'wholly superfluous' unpleasantness, and had set off home before us on foot. In his place, Zhitkov took a seat in our coach. The retired major wore a most dissatisfied expression, and kept twitching his moustaches like a spider.

'Well, your noble Excellency,' lisped Souvenir, 'is subordination exploded, eh? Wait a bit and see what will happen! They'll give you the sack too. Ah, a poor bridegroom you are, a poor bridegroom, an unlucky bride-groom!'

Souvenir was positively beside himself; while poor Zhitkov could do nothing but twitch his moustaches.

When I got home I told my mother all I had seen. She heard me to the end, and shook her head several times. 'It's a bad business,' was her comment. 'I don't like all these innovations!'

XV

Next day Martin Petrovitch came to dinner. My mother congratulated him on the successful conclusion of his project. 'You are now a free man,' she said, 'and ought to feel more at ease.'

'More at ease, to be sure, madam,' answered Martin Petrovitch, by no means, however, showing in the expression of his face that he really was more at ease. 'Now I can meditate upon my soul, and make ready for my last hour, as I ought.'

'Well,' queried my mother, 'and do the shooting pains still tingle in your arms?'

Harlov twice clenched and unclenched his left arm. 'They do, madam; and I've something else to tell you. As I begin to drop asleep, some one cries in my head, "Take care!" "Take care!"'

'That's nerves,' observed my mother, and she began speaking of the previous day, and referred to certain circumstances which had attended the completion of the deed of partition....

'To be sure, to be sure,' Harlov interrupted her, 'there was something of the sort... of no consequence. Only there's something I would tell you,' he added, hesitating—'I was not disturbed yesterday by Souvenir's silly words—even Mr. Attorney, though he's no fool—even he did not trouble me; no, it was quite another person disturbed me——' Here Harlov faltered.

'Who?' asked my mother.

Harlov fastened his eyes upon her: 'Evlampia!'

'Evlampia? Your daughter? How was that?'

'Upon my word, madam, she was like a stone! nothing

but a statue! Can it be she has no feeling? Her sister, Anna—well, she was all she should be. She's a keen-witted creature! But Evlampia—why, I'd shown her—I must own—so much partiality! Can it be she's no feeling for me! It's clear I'm in a bad way; it's clear I've a feeling that I'm not long for this world, since I make over everything to them; and yet she's like a stone! she might at least utter a sound! Bows—yes, she bows, but there's no thankfulness to be seen.'

'There, give over,' observed my mother, 'we'll marry her to Gavrila Fedulitch... she'll soon get softer in his hands.'

Martin Petrovitch once more looked from under his brows at my mother. 'Well, there's Gavrila Fedulitch, to be sure! You have confidence in him, then, madam?'

'I've confidence in him.'

'Very well; you should know best, to be sure. But Evlampia, let me tell you, is like me. The character is just the same. She has the wild Cossack blood, and her heart's like a burning coal!'

'Why, do you mean to tell me you've a heart like that, my dear sir?'

Harlov made no answer. A brief silence followed.

'What are you going to do, Martin Petrovitch,' my mother began, 'in what way do you mean to set about saving your soul now? Will you set off to Mitrophan or to Kiev, or may be you'll go to the Optin desert, as it's in the neighbourhood? There, they do say, there's a holy monk appeared... Father Makary they call him, no one remembers any one like him! He sees right through all sins.'

'If she really turns out an ungrateful daughter,' Harlov enunciated in a husky voice, 'then it would be better for me, I believe, to kill her with my own hands!'

'What are you saying! Lord, have mercy on you!' cried my mother. 'Think what you're saying! There, see, what a pretty pass it's come to. You should have listened to me the other day when you came to consult me! Now, here, you'll go tormenting yourself, instead of thinking of your soul! You'll be tormenting yourself, and all to no purpose! Yes! Here you're complaining now, and faint-hearted....'

This reproach seemed to stab Harlov to the heart. All his old pride came back to him with a rush. He shook himself, and thrust out his chin. 'I am not a man, madam, Natalia Nikolaevna, to complain or be faint-hearted,' he began sullenly. 'I simply wished to reveal my feelings to you as my benefactress and a person I respect. But the Lord God knows (here he raised his hand high above his head) that this globe of earth may crumble to pieces before I will go back from my word, or... (here he positively snorted) show a faint heart, or regret what I have done! I had good reasons, be sure! My daughters will never forget their duty, for ever and ever, amen!'

My mother stopped her ears. 'What's this for, my good sir, like a trumpet-blast! If you really have such faith in your family, well, praise the Lord for it! You've quite put my brains in a whirl!'

Martin Petrovitch begged pardon, sighed twice, and was silent. My mother once more referred to Kiev, the Optin desert, and Father Makary.... Harlov assented, said that 'he must... he must... he would have to... his soul ...' and that was all. He did not regain his cheerfulness before he went away. From time to time he clenched and unclenched his fist, looked at his open hand, said that what he feared above everything was dying without repentance, from a stroke, and that he had made a vow to himself not to get angry, as anger vitiated his blood and drove it to his head.... Besides, he had now withdrawn from everything. What grounds could he have for getting angry? Let other people trouble themselves now and vitiate their blood!

As he took leave of my mother he looked at her in a strange way, mournfully and questioningly... and suddenly, with a rapid movement, drew out of his pocket the volume of *The Worker's Leisure-Hour*, and thrust it into my mother's hand.

'What's that?' she inquired.

'Read... here,' he said hurriedly, 'where the corner's turned down, about death. It seems to me, it's terribly well said, but I can't make it out at all. Can't you explain it to me, my benefactress? I'll come back again and you explain it me.'

With these words Martin Petrovitch went away.

'He's in a bad way, he's in a bad way,' observed my mother, directly he had disappeared through the doorway, and she set to work upon the *Leisure-Hour*. On the page turned down by Harlov were the following words:

'Death is a grand and solemn work of nature. It is nothing else than that the spirit, inasmuch as it is lighter, finer, and infinitely more penetrating than those elements under whose sway it has been subject, nay, even than the force of electricity itself, so is chemically purified and striveth upward till what time it attaineth an equally spiritual abiding-place for itself ...' and so on.

My mother read this passage through twice, and exclaiming, 'Pooh!' she flung the book away.

Three days later, she received the news that her sister's husband was dead, and set off to her sister's country-seat, taking me with her. My mother proposed to spend a month with her, but she stayed on till late in the autumn, and it was only at the end of September that we returned to our own estate.

XVI

The first news with which my valet, Prokofy, greeted me
(he regarded himself as the seignorial huntsman) was
that there was an immense number of wild snipe on
the wing, and that in the birch-copse near Eskovo (Harlov's property), especially, they were simply swarming.
I had three hours before me till dinner-time. I promptly
seized my gun and my game-bag, and with Prokofy and
a setter-dog, hastened to the Eskovo copse. We certainly
did find a great many wild snipe there, and, firing about
thirty charges, killed five. As I hurried homewards with
my booty, I saw a peasant ploughing near the roadside. His horse had stopped, and with tearful and angry
abuse he was mercilessly tugging with the cord reins at
the animal's head, which was bent on one side. I looked
attentively at the luckless beast, whose ribs were all but
through its skin, and, bathed in sweat, heaved up and
down with convulsive, irregular movements like a black-
smith's bellows. I recognised it at once as the decrepit
old mare, with the scar on her shoulder, who had served
Martin Petrovitch so many years.

'Is Mr. Harlov living?' I asked Prokofy. The chase had
so completely absorbed us, that up to that instant we
had not talked of anything.

'Yes, he's alive. Why?'

'But that's his mare, isn't it? Do you mean to say he's
sold her?'

'His mare it is, to be sure; but as to selling, he never
sold her. But they took her away from him, and handed
her over to that peasant.'

'How, took it? And he consented?'

'They never asked his consent. Things have changed

here in your absence,' Prokofy observed. With a faint smile in response to my look of amazement; 'worse luck! My goodness, yes! Now Sletkin's master, and orders every one about.'

'But Martin Petrovitch?'

'Why, Martin Petrovitch has become the very last person here, you may say. He's on bread and water,— what more can one say? They've crushed him altogether. Mark my words; they'll drive him out of the house.'

The idea that it was possible to *drive* such a giant had never entered my head. 'And what does Zhitkov say to it?' I asked at last. 'I suppose he's married to the second daughter?'

'Married?' repeated Prokofy, and this time he grinned all over his face. 'They won't let him into the house. "We don't want you," they say; "get along home with you." It's as I said; Sletkin directs every one.'

'But what does the young lady say?'

'Evlampia Martinovna? Ah, master, I could tell you… but you're young—one must think of that. Things are going on here that are… oh!… oh!… oh! Hey! why Dianka's setting, I do believe!'

My dog actually had stopped short, before a thick oak bush which bordered a narrow ravine by the roadside. Prokofy and I ran up to the dog; a snipe flew up out of the bush, we both fired at it and missed; the snipe settled in another place; we followed it.

The soup was already on the table when I got back. My mother scolded me. 'What's the meaning of it?' she said with displeasure; 'the very first day, and you keep us waiting for dinner.' I brought her the wild snipe I had killed; she did not even look at them. There were also in the room Souvenir, Kvitsinsky, and Zhitkov. The retired major was huddled in a corner, for all the world like a schoolboy in disgrace. His face wore an expression of mingled confusion and annoyance; his eyes were red.... One might positively have imagined he had recently been in tears. My mother remained in an ill humour. I was at no great pains to surmise that my late arrival did not count for much in it. During dinner-time she hardly talked at all. The major turned beseeching glances upon her from time to time, but ate a good dinner nevertheless. Souvenir was all of a shake. Kvitsinsky preserved his habitual self-confidence of demeanour.

'Vikenty Osipitch,' my mother addressed him, 'I beg you to send a carriage tomorrow for Martin Petrovitch, since it has come to my knowledge that he has none of his own. And bid them tell him to come without fail, that I desire to see him.'

Kvitsinsky was about to make some rejoinder, but he restrained himself.

'And let Sletkin know,' continued my mother, 'that I command him to present himself before me.... Do you hear? I com... mand!'

'Yes, just so... that scoundrel ought——' Zhitkov was beginning in a subdued voice; but my mother gave him such a contemptuous look, that he promptly turned away and was silent.

'Do you hear? I command!' repeated my mother.

'Certainly, madam,' Kvitsinsky replied submissively but with dignity.

'Martin Petrovitch won't come!' Souvenir whispered to me, as he came out of the dining-room with me after dinner. 'You should just see what's happened to him! It's past comprehension! It's come to this, that whatever they say to him, he doesn't understand a word! Yes! They've got the snake under the pitch-fork!'

And Souvenir went off into his revolting laugh.

XVII

Souvenir's prediction turned out correct. Martin Petrovitch would not come to my mother. She was not at all
pleased with this, and despatched a letter to him. He
sent her a square bit of paper, on which the following
words were written in big letters: 'Indeed I can't. I should
die of shame. Let me go to my ruin. Thanks. Don't tor-
ture me.—Martin Harlov.' Sletkin did come, but not on
the day on which my mother had 'commanded' his
attendance, but twenty-four hours later. My mother gave
orders that he should be shown into her boudoir.... God
knows what their interview was about, but it did not
last long; a quarter of an hour, not more. Sletkin came
out of my mother's room, crimson all over, and with
such a viciously spiteful and insolent expression of face,
that, meeting him in the drawing-room, I was simply
petrified, while Souvenir, who was hanging about there,
stopped short in the middle of a snigger. My mother
came out of her boudoir, also very red in the face, and
announced, in the hearing of all, that Mr. Sletkin was
never, upon any pretext, to be admitted to her presence
again, and that if Martin Petrovitch's daughters were to
make bold—they've impudence enough, said she—to
present themselves, they, too, were to be refused admit-
tance. At dinner-time she suddenly exclaimed, 'The vile
little Jew! I picked him out of the gutter, I made him
a career, he owes everything, everything to me,—and
he dares to tell me I've no business to meddle in their
affairs! that Martin Petrovitch is full of whims and fancies,
and it's impossible to humour him! Humour him, indeed!
What a thing to say! Ah, he's an ungrateful wretch! An
insolent little Jew!'

Major Zhitkov, who happened to be one of the com-
pany at dinner, imagined that now it was no less than
the will of the Almighty for him to seize the opportunity

and put in his word... but my mother promptly settled
him. 'Well, and you're a fine one, too, my man!' she commented. 'Couldn't get the upper hand of a girl, and he
an officer! In command of a squadron! I can fancy how
it obeyed you! He take a steward's place indeed! a fine
steward he'd make!'

Kvitsinsky, who was sitting at the end of the table,
smiled to himself a little malignantly, while poor Zhitkov
could do nothing but twitch his moustaches, lift his eye-
brows, and bury the whole of his hirsute countenance
in his napkin.

After dinner, he went out on to the steps to smoke
his pipe as usual, and he struck me as so miserable and
forlorn, that, although I had never liked him, I joined
myself on to him at once.

'How was it, Gavrila Fedulitch,' I began without fur-
ther beating about the bush, 'that your affair with Evlampia Martinovna was broken off? I'd expected you to be
married long ago.'

The retired major looked at me dejectedly.

'A snake in the grass,' he began, uttering each letter
of each syllable with bitter distinctness, 'has poisoned
me with his fang, and turned all my hopes in life to
ashes. And I could tell you, Dmitri Semyonovitch, all his
hellish wiles, but I'm afraid of angering your mamma.'
('You're young yet'—Prokofy's expression flashed across
my mind.) 'Even as it is'——Zhitkov groaned.

'Patience... patience... nothing else is left me. (He
struck his fist upon his chest.) Patience, old soldier,
patience. I served the Tsar faithfully... honourably...
yes. I spared neither blood nor sweat, and now see what
I am brought to. Had it been in the regiment—and the
matter depending upon me,' he continued after a short
silence, spent in convulsively sucking at his cherrywood
pipe, 'I'd have... I'd have given it him with the flat side of

my sword... three times over... till he'd had enough....'

Zhitkov took the pipe out of his mouth, and fixed his eyes on vacancy, as though admiring the picture he had conjured up.

Souvenir ran up, and began quizzing the major. I turned away from them, and determined, come what may, I would see Martin Petrovitch with my own eyes.... My boyish curiosity was greatly stirred.

XVIII

Next day I set out with my gun and dog, but without Prokofy, to the Eskovo copse. It was an exquisite day; I fancy there are no days like that in September anywhere but in Russia. The stillness was such that one could hear, a hundred paces off, the squirrel hopping over the dry leaves, and the broken twig just feebly catching at the other branches, and falling, at last, on the soft grass—to lie there for ever, not to stir again till it rotted away. The air, neither warm nor chill, but only fragrant, and as it were keen, was faintly, deliciously stinging in my eyes and on my cheeks. A long spider-web, delicate as a silken thread, with a white ball in the middle, floated smoothly in the air, and sticking to the butt-end of my gun, stretched straight out in the air—a sign of settled and warm weather. The sun shone with a brightness as soft as moonlight. Wild snipe were to be met with pretty often; but I did not pay special attention to them. I knew that the copse went on almost to Harlov's home-stead, right up to the hedge of his garden, and I turned my steps in that direction, though I could not even imagine how I should get into the place itself, and was even doubtful whether I ought to try to do so, as my mother was so angry with its new owners. Sounds of life and humanity reached me from no great distance. I listened.... Some one was coming through the copse... straight towards me.

'You should have said so straight out, dear,' I heard a woman's voice.

'Be reasonable,' another voice broke in, the voice of a man. 'Can one do it all at once?'

I knew the voices. There was the gleam of a woman's blue gown through the reddening nut bushes. Beside it stood a dark full coat. Another instant—and there stepped out into the glade, five paces from me, Sletkin and Evlampia.

They were disconcerted at once. Evlampia promptly stepped back, away into the bushes. Sletkin thought a little, and came up to me. There was not a trace to be seen in his face of the obsequious meekness, with which he had paced up and down Harlov's courtyard, four months before, rubbing up my horse's snaffle. But neither could I perceive in it the insolent defiance, which had so struck me on the previous day, on the threshold of my mother's boudoir. It was still as white and pretty as ever, but seemed broader and more solid.

'Well, have you shot many snipe?' he asked me, raising his cap, smiling, and passing his hand over his black curls; 'you are shooting in our copse.... You are very welcome. We would not hinder you.... Quite the contrary.'

'I have killed nothing today,' I rejoined, answering his first question; 'and I will go out of your copse this instant.'

Sletkin hurriedly put on his cap. 'Indeed, why so? We would not drive you out—indeed, we're delighted.... Here's Evlampia Martinovna will say the same. Evlampia Martinovna, come here. Where have you hidden yourself?' Evlampia's head appeared behind the bushes. But she did not come up to us. She had grown prettier, and seemed taller and bigger than ever.

'I'm very glad, to tell the truth,' Sletkin went on, 'that I have met you. Though you are still young in years, you have plenty of good sense already. Your mother was pleased to be very angry with me yesterday—she would not listen to reason of any sort from me, but I declare, as before God, so before you now, I am not to blame in any way. We can't treat Martin Petrovitch otherwise than we do; he's fallen into complete dotage. One can't humour all his whims, really. But we show him all due respect. Only ask Evlampia Martinovna.'

Evlampia did not stir; her habitual scornful smile flickered about her lips, and her large eyes watched us with no friendly expression.

'But why, Vladimir Vassilievitch, have you sold Martin Petrovitch's mare?' (I was particularly impressed by that mare being in the possession of a peasant.)

'His mare, why did we sell it? Why, Lord have mercy on us—what use was she? She was simply eating her head off. But with the peasant she can work at the plough anyway. As for Martin Petrovitch, if he takes a fancy to drive out anywhere, he's only to ask us. We wouldn't refuse him a conveyance. On a holiday, we should be pleased.'

'Vladimir Vassilievitch,' said Evlampia huskily, as though calling him away, and she still did not stir from her place. She was twisting some stalks of ripple grass round her fingers and snapping off their heads, slapping them against each other.

'About the page Maximka again,' Sletkin went on, 'Martin Petrovitch complains because we've taken him away and apprenticed him. But kindly consider the matter for yourself. Why, what had he to do waiting on Martin Petrovitch? Kick up his heels; nothing more. And he couldn't even wait on him properly; on account of his stupidity and his youth. Now we have sent him away to a harness-maker's. He'll be turned into a first-rate handicraftsman—and make a good thing of it for himself—and pay us ransom-money too. And, living in a small way as we do, that's a matter of importance. On a little farm like ours, one can't afford to let anything slip.'

'And this is the man Martin Petrovitch called a "poor stick,"' I thought. 'But who reads to Martin Petrovitch now?' I asked.

'Why, what is there to read? He had one book—but, luckily, that's been mislaid somewhere.... And what use is reading at his age.'

'And who shaves him?' I asked again.

Sletkin gave an approving laugh, as though in response to an amusing joke. 'Why, nobody. At first he used to singe his beard in the candle—but now he lets it be altogether. And it's lovely!'

'Vladimir Vassilievitch!' Evlampia repeated insistently: 'Vladimir Vassilievitch!'

Sletkin made her a sign with his hand.

'Martin Petrovitch is clothed and cared for, and eats what we do. What more does he want? He declared himself that he wanted nothing more in this world but to think of his soul. If only he would realise that everything now, however you look at it, is ours. He says too that we don't pay him his allowance. But we've not always got money ourselves; and what does he want with it, when he has everything provided him? And we treat him as one of the family too. I'm telling you the truth. The rooms, for instance, which he occupies—how we need them! there's simply not room to turn round without them; but we don't say a word—we put up with it. We even think how to provide amusement for him. There, on St. Peter's Day, I bought him some excellent hooks in the town—real English ones, expensive hooks, to catch fish. There are lots of carp in our pond. Let him sit and fish; in an hour or two, there'd be a nice little fish soup provided. The most suitable occupation for old men.'

'Vladimir Vassilitch!' Evlampia called for the third time in an incisive tone, and she flung far away from her the grass she had been twisting in her fingers, 'I am going!' Her eyes met mine. 'I am going, Vladimir Vassilievitch!' she repeated, and vanished behind a bush.

'I'm coming, Evlampia Martinovna, directly!' shouted Sletkin. 'Martin Petrovitch himself agrees with us now,' he went on, turning again to me. 'At first he was offended, certainly, and even grumbled, until, you know, he realised; he was, you remember, a hot-tempered violent man—more's the pity! but there, he's grown quite meek now. Because he sees his own interest. Your mamma—mercy on us! how she pitched into me!... To be sure: she's a lady that sets as much store by her own authority as Martin Petrovitch used to do. But you come in and see for yourself. And you might put in a word when there's an opportunity. I feel Natalia Nikolaevna's bounty to me deeply. But we've got to live too.'

'And how was it Zhitkov was refused?' I asked.

'Fedulitch? That dolt?' Sletkin shrugged his shoulders. 'Why, upon my word, what use could he have been? His whole life spent among soldiers—and now he has a fancy to take up farming. He can keep the peasants up to the mark, says he, because he's been used to knocking men about. He can do nothing; even knocking men about wants some sense. Evlampia Martinovna refused him herself. He was a quite unsuitable person. All our farming would have gone to ruin with him!'

'Coo—y!' sounded Evlampia's musical voice.

'Coming! coming!' Sletkin called back. He held out his hand to me. Though unwillingly, I took it.

'I beg to take leave, Dmitri Semyonovitch,' said Sletkin, showing all his white teeth. 'Shoot wild snipe as much as you like. It's wild game, belonging to no one. But if you come across a hare—you spare it; that game is ours. Oh, and something else! won't you be having pups from your bitch? I should be obliged for one!'

'Coo—y!' Evlampia's voice rang out again.

'Coo—y!' Sletkin responded, and rushed into the bushes.

XIX

I remember, when I was left alone, I was absorbed in
wondering how it was Harlov had not pounded Sletkin
'into a jelly,' as he said, and how it was Sletkin had not
been afraid of such a fate. It was clear Martin Petrovitch really had grown 'meek,' I thought, and I had a still
stronger desire to make my way into Eskovo, and get
at least a glance at that colossus, whom I could never
picture to myself subdued and tractable. I had reached
the edge of the copse, when suddenly a big snipe, with
a great rush of wings, darted up at my very feet, and
flew off into the depths of the wood. I took aim; my
gun missed fire. I was greatly annoyed; it had been such
a fine bird, and I made up my mind to try if I couldn't
make it rise a second time. I set off in the direction of its
flight, and going some two hundred paces off into the
wood I caught sight—in a little glade, under an over-
hanging birch-tree—not of the snipe, but of the same
Sletkin once more. He was lying on his back, with both
hands under his head, and with smile of contentment
gazing upwards at the sky, swinging his left leg, which
was crossed over his right knee. He did not notice my
approach. A few paces from him, Evlampia was walking
slowly up and down the little glade, with downcast eyes.
It seemed as though she were looking for something in
the grass—mushrooms or something; now and then, she
stooped and stretched out her hand. She was singing in
a low voice. I stopped at once, and fell to listening. At
first I could not make out what it was she was singing,
but afterwards I recognised clearly the following well-
known lines of the old ballad:

'Hither, hither, threatening storm-cloud,

Slay for me the father-in-law,

Strike for me the mother-in-law,

The young wife I will kill myself!'

Evlampia sang louder and louder; the last words she delivered with peculiar energy. Sletkin still lay on his back and laughed to himself, while she seemed all the time to be moving round and round him.

'Oh, indeed!' he commented at last. 'The things that come into some people's heads!'

'What?' queried Evlampia.

Sletkin raised his head a little. 'What? Why, what words were those you were uttering?'

'Why, you know, Volodya, one can't leave the words out of a song,' answered Evlampia, and she turned and saw me. We both cried out aloud at once, and both rushed away in opposite directions.

I made my way hurriedly out of the copse, and crossing a narrow clearing, found myself facing Harlov's garden.

XX

I had no time, nor would it have been of any use, to deliberate over what I had seen. Only an expression kept recurring to my mind, 'love spell,' which I had lately heard, and over the signification of which I had pondered a good deal. I walked alongside the garden fence, and in a few moments, behind the silver poplars (they had not yet lost a single leaf, and the foliage was luxuriantly thick and brilliantly glistening), I saw the yard and two little lodges of Martin Petrovitch's homestead. The whole place struck me as having been tidied up and pulled into shape. On every side one could perceive traces of unflagging and severe supervision. Anna Martinovna came out on to the steps, and screwing up her blue-grey eyes, gazed for a long while in the direction of the copse.

'Have you seen the master?' she asked a peasant, who was walking across the yard.

'Vladimir Vassilitch?' responded the latter, taking his cap off. 'He went into the copse, surely.'

'I know, he went to the copse. Hasn't he come back? Haven't you seen him?'

'I've not seen him… nay.'

The peasant continued standing bareheaded before Anna Martinovna.

'Well, you can go,' she said. 'Or no——wait a bit—— where's Martin Petrovitch? Do you know?'

'Oh, Martin Petrovitch,' answered the peasant, in a sing-song voice, alternately lifting his right and then his left hand, as though pointing away somewhere, 'is sitting yonder, at the pond, with a fishing-rod. He's sitting in the reeds, with a rod. Catching fish, maybe, God knows.'

'Very well... you can go,' repeated Anna Martinovna; 'and put away that wheel, it's lying about.'

The peasant ran to carry out her command, while she remained standing a few minutes longer on the steps, still gazing in the direction of the copse. Then she clenched one fist menacingly, and went slowly back into the house. 'Axiutka!' I heard her imperious voice calling within.

Anna Martinovna looked angry, and tightened her lips, thin enough at all times, with a sort of special energy. She was carelessly dressed, and a coil of loose hair had fallen down on to her shoulder. But in spite of the negligence of her attire, and her irritable humour, she struck me, just as before, as attractive, and I should have been delighted to kiss the narrow hand which looked malignant too, as she twice irritably pushed back the loose tress.

XXI

'Can Martin Petrovitch have really taken to fishing?' I
asked myself, as I turned towards the pond, which was
on one side of the garden. I got on to the dam, looked
in all directions.... Martin Petrovitch was nowhere to
be seen. I bent my steps along one of the banks of the
pond, and at last, at the very top of it, in a little creek, in
the midst of flat broken-down stalks of reddish reed, I
caught sight of a huge greyish mass.... I looked intently:
it was Harlov. Bareheaded, unkempt, in a cotton smock
torn at the seams, with his legs crossed under him, he
was sitting motionless on the bare earth. So motionless
was he that a sandpiper, at my approach, darted up from
the dry mud a couple of paces from him, and flew with
a flash of its little wings and a whistle over the surface
of the water, showing that no one had moved to frighten
him for a long while. Harlov's whole appearance was
so extraordinary that my dog stopped short directly it
saw him, lifted its tail, and growled. He turned his head
a very little, and fixed his wild-looking eyes on me and
my dog. He was greatly changed by his beard, though it
was short, but thick and curly, in white tufts, like Astra-
chan fur. In his right hand lay the end of a rod, while
the other end hovered feebly over the water. I felt an
involuntary pang at my heart. I plucked up my spirits,
however, went up to him, and wished him good morning. He slowly blinked as though just awake.

'What are you doing, Martin Petrovitch,' I began,
'catching fish here?'

'Yes... fish,' he answered huskily, and pulled up the
rod, on which there fluttered a piece of line, a fathom
length, with no hook on it.

'Your tackle is broken off,' I observed, and noticed
the same moment that there was no sign of bait-tin nor

worms near Martin Petrovitch.... And what sort of fishing could there be in September?

'Broken off?' he said, and he passed his hand over his face. 'But it's all the same!'

He dropped the rod in again.

'Natalia Nikolaevna's son?' he asked me, after the lapse of two minutes, during which I had been gazing at him with secret bewilderment. Though he had grown terribly thinner, still he seemed a giant. But what rags he was dressed in, and how utterly he had gone to pieces altogether!

'Yes,' I answered, 'I'm the son of Natalia Nikolaevna B.'

'Is she well?'

'My mother is quite well. She was very much hurt at your refusal,' I added; 'she did not at all expect you would not wish to come and see her.'

Martin Petrovitch's head sank on his breast. 'Have you been there?' he asked, with a motion of his head.

'Where?'

'There, at the house. Haven't you? Go! What is there for you to do here? Go! It's useless talking to me. I don't like it.'

He was silent for a while.

'You'd like to be always idling about with a gun! In my young days I used to be inclined the same way too. Only my father was strict and made me respect him too. Mind you, very different from fathers nowadays. My father flogged me with a horsewhip, and that was the end of it! I'd to give up idling about! And so I respected him.... Oo!... Yes!...'

Harlov paused again.

'Don't you stop here,' he began again. 'You go along

to the house. Things are managed there now—it's first-rate. Volodka'.... Here he faltered for a second. 'Our Volodka's a good hand at everything. He's a fine fellow! yes, indeed, and a fine scoundrel too!'

I did not know what to say; Martin Petrovitch spoke very tranquilly.

'And you go and see my daughters. You remember, I daresay, I had daughters. They're managers too... clever ones. But I'm growing old, my lad; I'm on the shelf. Time to repose, you know....'

'Nice sort of repose!' I thought, glancing round. 'Martin Petrovitch!' I uttered aloud, 'you really must come and see us.'

Harlov looked at me. 'Go along, my lad, I tell you.'

'Don't hurt mamma's feelings; come and see us.'

'Go away, my lad, go away,' persisted Harlov. 'What do you want to talk to me for?'

'If you have no carriage, mamma will send you hers.'

'Go along!'

'But, really and truly, Martin Petrovitch!'

Harlov looked down again, and I fancied that his cheeks, dingy as though covered with earth, faintly flushed.

'Really, do come,' I went on. 'What's the use of your sitting here? of your making yourself miserable?'

'Making myself miserable?' he commented hesitatingly.

'Yes, to be sure—making yourself miserable!' I repeated.

Harlov said nothing, and seemed lost in musing. Emboldened by his silence, I determined to be open, to act straightforwardly, bluntly. (Do not forget, I was only fifteen then.)

'Martin Petrovitch!' I began, seating myself beside him. 'I know everything, you see, positively everything. I know how your son-in-law is treating you—doubtless with the consent of your daughters. And now you are in such a position.... But why lose heart?'

Harlov still remained silent, and simply dropped in his line; while I—what a sensible fellow, what a sage I felt!

'Doubtless,' I began again, 'you acted imprudently in giving up everything to your daughters. It was most generous on your part, and I am not going to blame you. In our days it is a quality only too rare! But since your daughters are so ungrateful, you ought to show a contempt—yes, a contempt—for them... and not fret——'

'Stop!' muttered Harlov suddenly, gnashing his teeth, and his eyes, staring at the pond, glittered wrathfully.... 'Go away!'

'But, Martin Petrovitch——'

'Go away, I tell you,... or I'll kill you!'

I had come quite close to him; but at the last words I instinctively jumped up. 'What did you say, Martin Petrovitch?'

'I'll kill you, I tell you; go away!' With a wild moan, a roar, the words broke from Harlov's breast, but he did not turn his head, and still stared wrathfully straight in front of him. 'I'll take you and fling you and your fool's counsel into the water. You shall learn to pester the old, little milksop!'

'He's gone mad!' flashed through my mind.

I looked at him more attentively, and was completely petrified; Martin Petrovitch was weeping!! Tear after tear rolled from his eyelashes down his cheeks... while his face had assumed an expression utterly savage....

'Go away!' he roared once more, 'or I'll kill you, by God! for an example to others!'

He was shaking all over from side to side, and showing his teeth like a wild boar. I snatched up my gun and took to my heels. My dog flew after me, barking. He, too, was frightened.

When I got home, I naturally did not, by so much as a word, to my mother, hint at what I had seen; but coming across Souvenir, I told him—the devil knows why—all about it. That loathsome person was so delighted at my story, shrieking with laughter, and even dancing with pleasure, that I could hardly forbear striking him.

'Ah! I should like,' he kept repeating breathless with laughter, 'to see that fiend, the Swede, Harlov, crawling into the mud and sitting in it....'

'Go over to the pond if you're so curious.'

'Yes; but how if he kills me?'

I felt horribly sick at Souvenir, and regretted my ill-timed confidence.... Zhitkov, to whom he repeated my tale, looked at the matter somewhat differently.

'We shall have to call in the police,' he concluded, 'or, may be, we may have to send for a battalion of military.'

His forebodings with regard to the military battalion did not come true; but something extraordinary really did happen.

XXII

In the middle of October, three weeks after my interview with Martin Petrovitch, I was standing at the window of my own room in the second storey of our house, and thinking of nothing at all, I looked disconsolately into the yard and the road that lay beyond it. The weather had been disgusting for the last five days. Shooting was not even to be thought of. All things living had hidden themselves; even the sparrows made no sound, and the rooks had long ago disappeared from sight. The wind howled drearily, then whistled spasmodically. The low-hanging sky, unbroken by one streak of light, had changed from an unpleasant whitish to a leaden and still more sinister hue; and the rain, which had been pouring and pouring, mercilessly and unceasingly, had suddenly become still more violent and more driving, and streamed with a rushing sound over the panes. The trees had been stripped utterly bare, and turned a sort of grey. It seemed they had nothing left to plunder; yet the wind would not be denied, but set to harassing them once more. Puddles, clogged with dead leaves, stood everywhere. Big bubbles, continually bursting and rising up again, leaped and glided over them. Along the roads, the mud lay thick and impassable. The cold pierced its way indoors through one's clothes to the very bones. An involuntary shiver passed over the body, and how sick one felt at heart! Sick, precisely, not sad. It seemed there would never again in the world be sunshine, nor brightness, nor colour, but this rain and mire and grey damp, and raw fog would last for ever, and for ever would the wind whine and moan! Well, I was standing moodily at my window, and I remember a sudden darkness came on—a bluish darkness—though the clock only pointed to twelve. Suddenly I fancied I saw a bear dash across our yard from the gates to the steps! Not on all-fours, certainly, but as he is depicted when he gets up on his hind-paws. I could not believe my eyes. If it were not a bear I had seen, it was, any way, something enormous, black shaggy.... I was still lost in wonder as to what it could be, when suddenly I heard below a furious knocking. It seemed something utterly unlooked for, something terrible was stumbling headlong into our house. Then began a commotion, a hurrying to and fro....

I quickly went down the stairs, ran into the dining-room....

At the drawing-room door facing me stood my mother, as though rooted to the spot. Behind her, peered several scared female faces. The butler, two footmen, and a page, with his mouth wide open with astonishment, were packed together in the doorway of the hall. In the middle of the dining-room, covered with mire, dishevelled, tattered, and soaking wet—so wet that steam rose all round and water was running in little streams over the floor—knelt, shaking ponderously, as it were, at the last gasp... the very monster I had seen dashing across the yard! And who was this monster? Harlov! I came up on one side, and saw, not his face, but his head, which he was clutching, with both hands in the hair that blinded him with filth. He was breathing heavily, brokenly; something positively rattled in his throat— and in all the bespattered dark mass, the only thing that could be clearly distinguished was the tiny whites of the eyes, straying wildly about. He was awful! The dignitary came into my mind whom he had once crushed for comparing him to a mastodon. Truly, so might have looked some antediluvian creature that had just escaped another more powerful monster, attacking it in the eternal slime of the primeval swamps.

'Martin Petrovitch!' my mother cried at last, and she clasped her hands. 'Is that you? Good God! Merciful heavens!'

'I... I ...' we heard a broken voice, which seemed with effort and painfully to dwell on each sound. 'Alas! It is I!'

'But what has happened to you? Mercy upon us!'

'Natalia Nikolaev... na... I have... run straight... to you... from home... on foot....'

'Through such mud! But you don't look like a man. Get up; sit down, anyway.... And you,' she turned to the maid-servants, 'run quick for cloths. And haven't you some dry clothes?' she asked the butler.

The butler gesticulated as though to say, Is it likely for such a size?... 'But we could get a coverlet,' he replied, 'or, there's a new horse-rug.'

'But get up, get up, Martin Petrovitch, sit down,' repeated my mother.

'They've turned me out, madam,' Harlov moaned suddenly, and he flung his head back and stretched his hands out before him. 'They've turned me out, Natalia Nikolaevna! My own daughters, out of my own home....'

My mother sighed and groaned.

'What are you saying? Turned you out! What wickedness! what wickedness!' (She crossed herself.) 'But do get up, Martin Petrovitch, I beg you!'

Two maid-servants came in with cloths and stood still before Harlov. It was clear they did not know how to attack this mountain of filth. 'They have turned me out, madam, they have turned me out!' Harlov kept repeating meanwhile. The butler returned with a large woollen coverlet, and he, too, stood still in perplexity. Souvenir's little head was thrust in at a door and vanished again.

'Martin Petrovitch! get up! Sit down! and tell me everything properly,' my mother commanded in a tone of determination.

Harlov rose.... The butler tried to assist him but only

dirtied his hand, and, shaking his fingers, retreated to the door. Staggering and faltering, Harlov got to a chair and sat down. The maids again approached him with their cloths, but he waved them off with his hand, and refused the coverlet. My mother did not herself, indeed, insist; to dry Harlov was obviously out of the question; they contented themselves with hastily wiping up his traces on the floor.

XXIII

'How have they turned you out?' my mother asked, as soon as he had a little time to recover himself.

'Madam! Natalia Nikolaevna!' he began, in a strained voice,—and again I was struck by the uneasy straying of his eyes; 'I will tell you the truth; I am myself most of all to blame.'

'Ay, to be sure; you would not listen to me at the time,' assented my mother, sinking into an arm-chair and slightly moving a scented handkerchief before her nose; very strong was the smell that came from Harlov... the odour in a forest bog is not so strong.

'Alas! that's not where I erred, madam, but through pride. Pride has been my ruin, as it ruined the Tsar Navuhodonosor. I fancied God had given me my full share of sense, and if I resolved on anything, it followed it was right; so... and then the fear of death came... I was utterly confounded! "I'll show," said I, "to the last, my power and my strength! I'll bestow all on them,— and they must feel it all their lives...."' (Harlov suddenly was shaking all over....) 'Like a mangy dog they have driven me out of the house! This is their gratitude!'

'In what way——,' my mother was beginning....

'They took my page, Maximka, from me,' Harlov interrupted her (his eyes were still wandering, he held both hands—the fingers interlaced—under his chin), 'my carriage they took away, my monthly allowance they cut down, did not pay me the sum specified, cut me short all round, in fact; still I said nothing, bore it all! And I bore it by reason... alas! of my pride again. That my cruel enemies might not say, "See, the old fool's sorry for it now"; and you too, do you remember, madam, had warned me; "mind you, it's all to no purpose," you said!

and so I bore it.... Only, today I came into my room, and it was occupied already, and my bed they'd thrown out into the lumber-room! "You can sleep there; we put up with you there even only out of charity; we've need of your room for the household." And this was said to me by whom? Volodka Sletkin! the vile hound, the base cur!'

Harlov's voice broke.

'But your daughters? What did they do?' asked my mother.

'But I bore it all,' Harlov went on again; 'bitterness, bitterness was in my heart, let me tell you, and shame.... I could not bear to look upon the light of day! That was why I was unwilling to come and see you, ma'am, from this same feeling, from shame for my disgrace! I have tried everything, my good friend; kindness, affection, and threats, and I reasoned with them, and more besides! I bowed down before them... like this.' (Harlov showed how he had bowed down.) 'And all in vain. And all of it I bore! At the beginning, at first, I'd very different thoughts; I'll up, I thought, and kill them. I'll crush them all, so that not a trace remains of them!... I'll let them know! Well, but after, I submitted! It's a cross, I thought, laid upon me; it's to bid me make ready for death. And all at once, today, driven out, like a cur! And by whom? Volodka! And you asked about my daughters; they've no will of their own at all. They're Volodka's slaves! Yes!'

My mother wondered. 'In Anna's case I can understand that; she's a wife.... But how comes it your second....'

'Evlampia? She's worse than Anna! She's altogether given herself up into Volodka's hands. That's the reason she refused your soldier, too. At his, at Volodka's bidding. Anna, to be sure, ought to resent it, and she can't bear her sister, but she submits! He's bewitched them, the cursed scoundrel! Though she, Anna, I daresay, is pleased to think that Evlampia, who was always so proud,—and now see what she's come to!... O... alas... alas! God, my God!'

My mother looked uneasily towards me. I moved a little away as a precautionary measure, for fear I should be sent away altogether....

'I am very sorry indeed, Martin Petrovitch,' she began, 'that my former protégé has caused you so much sorrow, and has turned out so badly. But I, too, was mistaken in him.... Who could have expected this of him?'

'Madam,' Harlov moaned out, and he struck himself a blow on the chest, 'I cannot bear the ingratitude of my daughters! I cannot, madam! You know I gave them everything, everything! And besides, my conscience has been tormenting me. Many things... alas! many things I have thought over, sitting by the pond, fishing. "If you'd only done good to any one in your life!" was what I pondered upon, "succoured the poor, set the peasants free, or something, to atone for having wrung their lives out of them. You must answer for them before God! Now their tears are revenged." And what sort of life have they now? It was a deep pit even in my time—why disguise my sins?—but now there's no seeing the bottom! All these sins I have taken upon my soul; I have sacrificed my conscience for my children, and for this I'm laughed to scorn! Kicked out of the house, like a cur!'

'Don't think about that, Martin Petrovitch,' observed my mother.

'And when he told me, your Volodka,' Harlov went on with fresh force, 'when he told me I was not to live in my room any more,—I laid every plank in that room with my own hands,—when he said that to me,—God only knows what passed within me! It was all confusion in my head, and like a knife in my heart.... Either to cut his throat or get away out of the house!... So, I have run to you, my benefactress, Natalia Nikolaevna... where had I to lay my head? And then the rain, the filth... I fell down twenty times, maybe! And now... in such unseemly....'

Harlov scanned himself and moved restlessly in his chair, as though intending to get up.

'Say no more, Martin Petrovitch,' my mother interposed hurriedly; 'what does that signify? That you've made the floor dirty? That's no great matter! Come, I want to make you a proposition. Listen! They shall take you now to a special room, and make you up a clean bed,—you undress, wash, and lie down and sleep a little....'

'Natalia Nikolaevna! There's no sleeping for me!' Harlov responded drearily. 'It's as though there were hammers beating in my brain! Me! like some good-for-nothing beast!...'

'Lie down and sleep,' my mother repeated insistently. 'And then we'll give you some tea,—yes, and we'll have a talk. Don't lose heart, old friend! If they've driven you out of *your* house, in *my* house you will always find a home.... I have not forgotten, you know, that you saved my life.'

'Benefactress!' moaned Harlov, and he covered his face with his hand. '*You* must save me now!'

This appeal touched my mother almost to tears. 'I am ready and eager to help you, Martin Petrovitch, in everything I am able. But you must promise me that you will listen to me in future and dismiss every evil thought from you.'

Harlov took his hands from his face. 'If need be,' he said, 'I can forgive them, even!'

My mother nodded her head approvingly. 'I am very glad to see you in such a truly Christian frame of mind, Martin Petrovitch; but we will talk of that later. Meanwhile, you put yourself to rights, and, most of all, sleep. Take Martin Petrovitch to what was the master's room, the green room,' said my mother, addressing the butler, 'and whatever he asks for, let him have it on the spot! Give orders for his clothes to be dried and washed, and ask the housekeeper for what linen is needed. Do you hear?'

'Yes, madam,' responded the butler.

'And as soon as he's asleep, tell the tailor to take his measure; and his beard will have to be shaved. Not at once, but after.'

'Yes, madam,' repeated the butler. 'Martin Petrovitch, kindly come.' Harlov got up, looked at my mother, was about to go up to her, but stopped, swinging a bow from the waist, crossed himself three times to the image, and followed the steward. Behind him, I, too, slipped out of the room.

XXIV

The butler conducted Harlov to the green room, and at once ran off for the wardroom maid, as it turned out there were no sheets on the bed. Souvenir, who met us in the passage, and popped into the green room with us, promptly proceeded to dance, grinning and chuckling, round Harlov, who stood, his arms held a little away from him, and his legs apart, in the middle of the room, seeming lost in thought. The water was still dripping from him.

'The Swede! The Swede, Harlus!' piped Souvenir, doubling up and holding his sides. 'Mighty founder of the illustrious race of Harlovs, look down on thy descendant! What does he look like? Dost thou recognise him? Ha, ha, ha! Your excellency, your hand, I beg; why, have you got on black gloves?'

I tried to restrain Souvenir, to put him to shame... but it was too late for that now.

'He called me parasite, toady! "You've no roof," said he, "to call your own." But now, no doubt about it, he's become as dependent as poor little me. Martin Petrovitch and Souvenir, the poor toady, are equal now. He'll have to live on charity too. They'll toss him the stale and dirty crust, that the dog has sniffed at and refused.... And they'll tell him to eat it, too. Ha, ha, ha!'

Harlov still stood motionless, his head drawn in, his legs and arms held a little apart.

'Martin Harlov, a nobleman born!' Souvenir went on shrieking. 'What airs he used to give himself. Just look at me! Don't come near, or I'll knock you down!... And when he was so clever as to give away and divide his property, didn't he crow! "Gratitude!..." he cackled, "gratitude!" But why were you so mean to me? Why

didn't you make me a present? May be, I should have
felt it more. And you see I was right when I said they'd
strip you bare, and....'

'Souvenir!' I screamed; but Souvenir was in nowise
daunted. Harlov still did not stir. It seemed as though
he were only now beginning to be aware how soaking
wet everything was that he had on, and was waiting to
be helped off with his clothes. But the butler had not
come back.

'And a military man too!' Souvenir began again. 'In the
year twelve, he saved his country; he showed proofs of
his valour. I see how it is. Stripping the frozen marauders
of their breeches is work he's quite equal to, but
when the hussies stamp their feet at him he's frightened
out of his skin.'

'Souvenir!' I screamed a second time.

Harlov looked askance at Souvenir. Till that instant he
seemed not to have noticed his presence, and only my
exclamation aroused his attention.

'Look out, brother,' he growled huskily, 'don't dance
yourself into trouble.'

Souvenir fairly rolled about with laughter. 'Ah, how
you frighten me, most honoured brother. You're a formidable
person, to be sure. You must comb your hair,
at any rate, or, God forbid, it'll get dry, and you'll never
wash it clean again; you'll have to mow it with a sickle.'
Souvenir all of a sudden got into a fury. 'And you give
yourself airs still. A poor outcast, and he gives himself
airs. Where's your home now? you'd better tell me that,
you were always boasting of it. "I have a home of my
own," he used to say, but you're homeless. "My ancestral
roof," he would say.' Souvenir pounced on this phrase
as an inspiration.

'Mr. Bitchkov,' I protested. 'What are you about? you
forget yourself.'

But he still persisted in chattering, and still danced and pranced up and down quite close to Harlov. And still the butler and the wardroom maid did not come.

I felt alarmed. I began to notice that Harlov, who had, during his conversation with my mother, gradually grown quieter, and even towards the end apparently resigned himself to his fate, was beginning to get worked up again. He breathed more hurriedly, it seemed as though his face were suddenly swollen under his ears, his fingers twitched, his eyes again began moving restlessly in the dark mask of his grim face....

'Souvenir, Souvenir!' I cried. 'Stop it, I'll tell mamma.'

But Souvenir seemed possessed by frenzy. 'Yes, yes, most honoured brother,' he began again, 'here we find ourselves, you and I, in the most delicate position. While your daughters, with your son-in-law, Vladimir Vassilievitch, are having a fine laugh at you under your roof. And you should at least curse them, as you promised. Even that you're not equal to. To be sure, how could you hold your own with Vladimir Vassilievitch? Why, you used to call him Volodka, too. You call him Volodka. *He* is Vladimir Vassilievitch, Mr. Sletkin, a landowner, a gentleman, while—what are you, pray?'

A furious roar drowned Souvenir's words.... Harlov was aroused. His fists were clenched and lifted, his face was purple, there was foam on his drawn lips, he was shaking with rage. 'Roof, you say!' he thundered in his iron voice, 'curse, you say.... No! I will not curse them.... They don't care for that.... But the roof... I will tear the roof off them, and they shall have no roof over their heads, like me. They shall learn to know Martin Harlov. My strength is not all gone yet; they shall learn to laugh at me!... They shall have no roof over their heads!'

I was stupefied; never in my life had I witnessed such boundless anger. Not a man—a wild beast—paced to and fro before me. I was stupefied... as for Souvenir, he had hidden under the table in his fright.

'They shall not!' Harlov shouted for the last time, and almost knocking over the butler and the wardroom maid, he rushed away out of the house.... He dashed headlong across the yard, and vanished through the gates.

XXV

My mother was terribly angry when the butler came with an abashed countenance to report Martin Petrovitch's sudden and unexpected retreat. He did not dare to conceal the cause of this retreat; I was obliged to confirm his story. 'Then it was all your doing!' my mother cried, at the sight of Souvenir, who had run in like a hare, and was even approaching to kiss her hand: 'Your vile tongue is to blame for it all!' 'Excuse me, d'rectly, d'rectly ...' faltered Souvenir, stuttering and drawing back his elbows behind him. 'D'rectly,... d'rectly... I know your "d'rectly,"' my mother repeated reprovingly, and she sent him out of the room. Then she rang the bell, sent for Kvitsinsky, and gave him orders to set off on the spot to Eskovo, with a carriage, to find Martin Petrovitch at all costs, and to bring him back. 'Do not let me see you without him,' she concluded. The gloomy Pole bowed his head without a word, and went away.

I went back to my own room, sat down again at the window, and I pondered a long while, I remember, on what had taken place before my eyes. I was puzzled; I could not understand how it was that Harlov, who had endured the insults of his own family almost without a murmur, had lost all self-control, and been unable to put up with the jeers and pin-pricks of such an abject creature as Souvenir. I did not understand in those days what insufferable bitterness there may sometimes be in a foolish taunt, even when it comes from lips one scorns.... The hated name of Sletkin, uttered by Souvenir, had been like a spark thrown into powder. The sore spot could not endure this final prick.

About an hour passed by. Our coach drove into the yard; but our steward sat in it alone. And my mother had said to him—'don't let me see you without him.'

Kvitsinsky jumped hurriedly out of the carriage, and ran up the steps. His face had a perturbed look—something very unusual with him. I promptly rushed downstairs, and followed at his heels into the drawing-room. 'Well? have you brought him?' asked my mother.

'I have not brought him,' answered Kvitsinsky—'and I could not bring him.'

'How's that? Have you seen him?'

'Yes.'

'What has happened to him? A fit?'

'No; nothing has happened.'

'How is it you didn't bring him?'

'He's pulling his house to pieces.'

'What?'

'He's standing on the roof of the new building, and pulling it to pieces. Forty boards or more, I should guess, must have come down by now, and some five of the rafters too.' ('They shall not have a roof over their heads.' Harlov's words came back to me.)

My mother stared at Kvitsinsky. 'Alone… he's standing on the roof, and pulling the roof down?'

'Exactly so. He is walking about on the flooring of the garret in the roof, and smashing right and left of him. His strength, you are aware, madam, is superhuman. And the roof too, one must say, is a poor affair; half-inch deal battens, laid wide apart, one inch nails.'

My mother looked at me, as though wishing to make sure whether she had heard aright. 'Half-inches wide apart,' she repeated, obviously not understanding the meaning of one word. 'Well, what then?' she said at last.

'I have come for instructions. There's no doing anything without men to help. The peasants there are all limp with fright.'

'And his daughters—what of them?'

'His daughters are doing nothing. They're running to and fro, shouting... this and that... all to no purpose.'

'And is Sletkin there?'

'He's there too. He's making more outcry than all of them—but he can't do anything.'

'And Martin Petrovitch is standing on the roof?'

'On the roof... that is, in the garret—and pulling the roof to pieces.'

'Yes, yes,' said my mother, 'half-inches wide apart.'

The position was obviously a serious one. What steps were to be taken? Send to the town for the police captain? Get together the peasants? My mother was quite at her wits' end. Zhitkov, who had come in to dinner, was nonplussed too. It is true, he made another reference to a battalion of military; he offered no advice, however, but confined himself to looking submissive and devoted. Kvitsinsky, seeing he would not get at any instructions, suggested to my mother—with the contemptuous respectfulness peculiar to him—that if she would authorise him to take a few of the stable-boys, gardeners, and other house-serfs, he would make an effort....

'Yes, yes,' my mother cut him short, 'do make an effort, dear Vikenty Osipitch! Only make haste, please, and I will take all responsibility on myself!'

Kvitsinsky smiled coldly. 'One thing let me make clear, madam, beforehand; it's impossible to reckon on any result, seeing that Mr. Harlov's strength is so great, and he is so desperate too; he feels himself to have been very cruelly wronged!'

'Yes, yes,' my mother assented; 'and it's all that vile Souvenir's fault! Never will I forgive him for it. Go and take the servants and set off, Vikenty Osipitch!'

'You'd better take plenty of cord, Mr. Steward, and some fire-escape tackle,' Zhitkov brought out in his bass—'and if there is such a thing as a net, it would be as well to take that along too. We once had in our regiment....'

'Kindly refrain from instructing me, sir,' Kvitsinsky cut him short, with an air of vexation; 'I know what is needed without your aid.'

Zhitkov was offended, and protested that as he imagined he, too, was called upon....

'No, no!' interposed my mother; 'you'd better stop where you are.... Let Vikenty Osipitch act alone.... Make haste, Vikenty Osipitch!'

Zhitkov was still more offended, while Kvitsinsky bowed and went out.

I rushed off to the stable, hurriedly saddled my horse myself, and set off at a gallop along the road to Eskovo.

XXVI

The rain had ceased, but the wind was blowing with redoubled force—straight into my face. Half-way there, the saddle almost slipped round under me; the girth had got loose; I got off and tried to tighten the straps with my teeth.... All at once I heard someone calling me by my name.... Souvenir was running towards me across the green fields. 'What!' he shouted to me from some way off, 'was your curiosity too much for you? But it's no use.... I went over there, straight, at Harlov's heels.... Such a state of things you never saw in your life!'

'You want to enjoy what you have done,' I said indignantly, and, jumping on my horse, I set off again at a gallop. But the indefatigable Souvenir did not give me up, and chuckled and grinned, even as he ran. At last, Eskovo was reached—there was the dam, and there the long hedge and willow-tree of the homestead.... I rode up to the gate, dismounted, tied up my horse, and stood still in amazement.

Of one third of the roof of the newer house, of the front part, nothing was left but the skeleton; boards and litter lay in disorderly heaps on the ground on both sides of the building. Even supposing the roof to be, as Kvitsinsky had said, a poor affair, even so, it was something incredible! On the floor of the garret, in a whirl of dust and rubbish, a blackish grey mass was moving to and fro with rapid ungainly action, at one moment shaking the remaining chimney, built of brick, (the other had fallen already) then tearing up the boarding and flinging it down below, then clutching at the very rafters. It was Harlov. He struck me as being exactly like a bear at this moment too; the head, and back, and shoulders were a bear's, and he put his feet down wide apart without bending the insteps—also like a bear. The bitter wind was blowing upon him from every side, lifting his matted locks. It was horrible to see, here and there, red patches of bare flesh through the rents in his tattered clothes; it was horrible to hear his wild husky muttering. There were a lot of people in the yard; peasant-women, boys, and servant-girls stood close along the hedge. A few peasants huddled together in a separate group, a little way off. The old village priest, whom I knew, was standing, bareheaded, on the steps of the other house, and holding a brazen cross in both hands, from time to time, silently and hopelessly, raised it, and, as it were, showed it to Harlov. Beside the priest, stood Evlampia with her back against the wall, gazing fixedly at her father. Anna, at one moment, pushed her head out of the little window, then vanished, then hurried into the yard, then went back into the house. Sletkin—pale all over, livid—in an old dressing-gown and smoking-cap, with a single-barrelled rifle in his hands, kept running to and fro with little steps. He had completely *gone Jewish*, as it is called. He was gasping, threatening, shaking, pointing the gun at Harlov, then letting it drop back on his shoulder—pointing it again, shrieking, weeping.... On seeing Souvenir and me he simply flew to us.

'Look, look, what is going on here!' he wailed—'look! He's gone out of his mind, he's raving mad... and see what he's doing! I've sent for the police already—but no one comes! No one comes! If I do fire at him, the law couldn't touch me, for every man has a right to defend his own property! And I will fire!... By God, I'll fire!'

He ran off toward the house.

'Martin Petrovitch, look out! If you don't get down, I'll fire!'

'Fire away!' came a husky voice from the roof. 'Fire away! And meanwhile here's a little present for you!'

A long plank flew up, and, turning over twice in the air, came violently to the earth, just at Sletkin's feet. He positively jumped into the air, while Harlov chuckled.

'Merciful Jesus!' faltered some one behind me. I looked round: Souvenir. 'Ah!' I thought, 'he's left off laughing now!'

Sletkin clutched a peasant, who was standing near, by the collar.

'Climb up now, climb up, climb up, all of you, you devils,' he wailed, shaking the man with all his force, 'save my property!'

The peasant took a couple of steps forward, threw his head back, waved his arms, shouted—'hi! here! master!' shifted from one foot to the other uneasily, and then turned back.

'A ladder! bring a ladder!' Sletkin addressed the other peasants.

'Where are we to get it?' was heard in answer.

'And if we had a ladder,' one voice pronounced deliberately, 'who'd care to climb up? Not such fools! He'd wring your neck for you—in a twinkling!'

'He'd kill one in no time,' said one young lad with flaxen hair and a half-idiotic face.

'To be sure he would,' the others confirmed. It struck me that, even if there had been no obvious danger, the peasants would yet have been loath to carry out their new owner's orders. They almost approved of Harlov, though they were amazed at him.

'Ugh, you robbers!' moaned Sletkin; 'you shall all catch it....'

But at this moment, with a heavy rumble, the last chimney came crashing down, and, in the midst of the cloud of yellow dust that flew up instantly, Harlov—uttering a piercing shriek and lifting his bleeding hands high in the air—turned facing us. Sletkin pointed the gun at him again.

95

Evlampia pulled him back by the elbow.

'Don't interfere!' he snarled savagely at her.

'And you—don't you dare!' she answered; and her blue eyes flashed menacingly under her scowling brows. 'Father's pulling his house down. It's his own.'

'You lie: it's ours!'

'You say ours; but I say it's his.'

Sletkin hissed with fury; Evlampia's eyes seemed stabbing him in the face.

'Ah, how d'ye do! my delightful daughter!' Harlov thundered from above. 'How d'ye do! Evlampia Martinovna! How are you getting on with your sweetheart? Are your kisses sweet, and your fondling?'

'Father!' rang out Evlampia's musical voice.

'Eh, daughter?' answered Harlov; and he came down to the very edge of the wall. His face, as far as I could make it out, wore a strange smile, a bright, mirthful—and for that very reason peculiarly strange and evil—smile.... Many years later I saw just the same smile on the face of a man condemned to death.

'Stop, father; come down. We are in fault; we give everything back to you. Come down.'

'What do you mean by disposing of what's ours?' put in Sletkin. Evlampia merely scowled more angrily.

'I give you back my share. I give up everything. Give over, come down, father! Forgive us; forgive me.'

Harlov still went on smiling. 'It's too late, my darling,' he said, and each of his words rang out like brass. 'Too late your stony heart is touched! The rock's started rolling downhill—there's no holding it back now! And don't look to me now; I'm a doomed man! You'd do better to look to your Volodka; see what a pretty fellow you've picked out! And look to your hellish sister; there's her foxy nose yonder thrust out of the window; she's peering yonder after that husband of hers! No, my good friends; you would rob me of a roof over my head, so I will leave you not one beam upon another! With my own hands I built it, with my own hands I destroy it,—yes, with my hands alone! See, I've taken no axe to help me!'

He snorted at his two open hands, and clutched at the centre beam again.

'Enough, father,' Evlampia was saying meanwhile, and her voice had grown marvellously caressing, 'let bygones be bygones. Come, trust me; you always trusted me. Come, get down; come to me to my little room, to my soft bed. I will dry you and warm you; I will bind up your wounds; see, you have torn your hands. You shall live with me as in Christ's bosom; food shall be sweet to you—and sleep sweeter yet. Come, we have done wrong! yes, we were puffed up, we have sinned; come, forgive!'

Harlov shook his head. 'Talk away! Me believe you! Never again! You've murdered all trust in my heart! You've murdered everything! I was an eagle, and became a worm for you... and you,—would you even crush the worm? Have done! I loved you, you know very well,—but now you are no daughter to me, and I'm no father to you... I'm a doomed man! Don't meddle! As for you, fire away, coward, mighty man of valour!' Harlov bellowed suddenly at Sletkin. 'Why is it you keep aiming and don't shoot? Are you mindful of the law; if the recipient of a gift commits an attempt upon the life of the giver,' Harlov enunciated distinctly, 'then the giver is empowered to claim everything back again? Ha, ha! don't be afraid, law-abiding man! I'd make no claims. I'll make an end of everything myself.... Here goes!'

'Father!' for the last time Evlampia besought him.

'Silence!'

'Martin Petrovitch! brother, be generous and forgive!' faltered Souvenir.

'Father! dear father!'

'Silence, bitch!' shouted Harlov. At Souvenir he did not even glance,—he merely spat in his direction.

XXVII

At that instant, Kvitsinsky, with all his retinue—in three carts—appeared at the gates. The tired horses panted, the men jumped out, one after another, into the mud.

'Aha!' Harlov shouted at the top of his voice. 'An army... here it comes, an army! A whole army they're sending against me! Capital! Only I give warning—if any one comes up here to me on the roof, I'll send him flying down, head over heels! I'm an inhospitable master; I don't like visitors at wrong times! No indeed!'

He was hanging with both hands on to the front rafters of the roof, the so-called standards of the gable, and beginning to shake them violently. Balancing on the edge of the garret flooring, he dragged them, as it were, after him, chanting rhythmically like a bargeman, 'One more pull! one more! o-oh!'

Sletkin ran up to Kvitsinsky and was beginning to whimper and pour out complaints.... The latter begged him 'not to interfere,' and proceeded to carry out the plan he had evolved. He took up his position in front of the house, and began, by way of diversion, to explain to Harlov that what he was about was unworthy of his rank....

'One more pull! one more!' chanted Harlov.

... 'That Natalia Nikolaevna was greatly displeased at his proceedings, and had not expected it of him....'

'One more pull! one more! o-oh!' Harlov chanted... while, meantime, Kvitsinsky had despatched the four sturdiest and boldest of the stable-boys to the other side of the house to clamber up the roof from behind. Harlov, however, detected the plan of attack; he suddenly left the standards and ran quickly to the back part of the roof. His appearance was so alarming that the two stable-boys who had already got up to the garret, dropped instantly back again to the ground by the water-pipe, to the great glee of the serf boys, who positively roared with laughter. Harlov shook his fist after them and, going back to the front part of the house, again clutched at the standards and began once more loosening them, singing again, like a bargeman.

Suddenly he stopped, stared....

'Maximushka, my dear! my friend!' he cried; 'is it you?'

I looked round.... There, actually, was Maximka, stepping out from the crowd of peasants. Grinning and showing his teeth, he walked forward. His master, the tailor, had probably let him come home for a holiday.

'Climb up to me, Maximushka, my faithful servant,' Harlov went on; 'together let us rid ourselves of evil Tartar folk, of Lithuanian thieves!'

Maximka, still grinning, promptly began climbing up the roof.... But they seized him and pulled him back—goodness knows why; possibly as an example to the rest; he could hardly have been much aid to Martin Petrovitch.

'Oh, all right! Good!' Harlov pronounced, in a voice of menace, and again he took hold of the standards.

'Vikenty Osipovitch! with your permission, I'll shoot,' Sletkin turned to Kvitsinsky; 'more to frighten him, see, than anything; my gun's only charged with snipe-shot.' But Kvitsinsky had not time to answer him, when the front couple of standards, viciously shaken in Harlov's iron hands, heeled over with a loud crack and crashed into the yard; and with it, not able to stop himself, came Harlov too, and fell with a heavy thud on the earth. Every one shuddered and drew a deep breath.... Harlov lay without stirring on his breast, and on his back lay the top central beam of the roof, which had come down with the falling gable's timbers.

XXVIII

They ran up to Harlov, rolled the beam off him, turned him over on his back. His face was lifeless, there was blood about his mouth; he did not seem to breathe. 'The breath is gone out of him,' muttered the peasants, standing about him. They ran to the well for water, brought a whole bucketful, and drenched Harlov's head. The mud and dust ran off his face, but he looked as lifeless as ever. They dragged up a bench, set it in the house itself, and with difficulty raising the huge body of Martin Petrovitch, laid it there with the head to the wall. The page Maximka approached, fell on one knee, and, his other leg stretched far behind him, in a theatrical way, supported his former master's arm. Evlampia, pale as death, stood directly facing her father, her great eyes fastened immovably upon him. Anna and Sletkin did not come near him. All were silent, all, as it were, waited for something. At last we heard broken, smacking noises in Harlov's throat, as though he were swallowing.... Then he feebly moved one, his right, hand (Maximka supported the left), opened one, the right eye, and slowly gazing about him, as though drunken with some fearful drunkenness, groaned, articulated, stammering, 'I'm sma-ashed ...' and as though after a moment's thought, added, 'here it is, the ra... aven co... olt!' The blood suddenly gushed thickly from his mouth... his whole body began to quiver....

'The end!' I thought.... But once more Harlov opened the same eye (the left eyelid lay as motionless as on a dead man's face), and fixing it on Evlampia, he articulated, hardly above a breath, 'Well, daugh... ter... you, I do not....'

Kvitsinsky, with a sharp motion of his hand, beckoned to the priest, who was still standing on the step.... The old man came up, his narrow cassock clinging about his feeble knees. But suddenly there was a sort of horrible twitching in Harlov's legs and in his stomach too; an irregular contraction passed upwards over his face. Evlampia's face seemed quivering and working in the same way. Maximka began crossing himself.... I was seized with horror; I ran out to the gates, squeezed myself close to them, not looking round. A minute later a soft murmur ran through the crowd, behind my back, and I understood that Martin Petrovitch was no more.

His skull had been fractured by the beam and his ribs injured, as it appeared at the post-mortem examination.

XXIX

What had he wanted to say to her as he lay dying? I
asked myself as I went home on my cob: 'I do not...
forgive,' or 'do not... pardon.' The rain had come on
again, but I rode at a walking pace. I wanted to be alone
as long as possible; I wanted to give myself up to my
reflections, unchecked. Souvenir had gone back in one
of the carts that had come with Kvitsinsky. Young and
frivolous as I was at that time, the sudden sweeping
change (not in mere details only) that is invariably called
forth in all hearts by the coming of death—expected
or unexpected, it makes no difference!—its majesty, its
gravity, and its truthfulness could not fail to impress me.
I was impressed too,... but for all that, my troubled,
childish eyes noted many things at once; they noted
how Sletkin, hurriedly and furtively, as though it were
something stolen, popped the gun out of sight; how he
and his wife became, both of them, instantly the object
of a sort of unspoken but universal aloofness. To Evlampia, though her fault was probably no less than her sister's, this aloofness did not extend. She even aroused a
certain sympathy, when she fell at her dead father's feet.
But that she too was guilty, that was none the less felt by
all. 'The old man was wronged,' said a grey-haired peasant with a big head, leaning, like some ancient judge,
with both hands and his beard on a long staff; 'on your
soul lies the sin! You wronged him!' That saying was at
once accepted by every one as the final judgment. The
peasants' sense of justice found expression in it, I felt
that at once. I noticed too that, at the first, Sletkin did
not *dare* to give directions. Without him, they lifted up
the body and carried it into the other house. Without
asking him, the priest went for everything needful to
the church, while the village elder ran to the village to
send off a cart and horse to the town. Even Anna Mar-

tinovna did not venture to use her ordinary imperious tone in ordering the samovar to be brought, 'for hot water, to wash the deceased.' Her orders were more like an entreaty, and she was answered rudely....

I was absorbed all the while by the question, What was it exactly he wanted to say to his daughter? Did he want to forgive her or to curse her? Finally I decided that it was—forgiveness.

Three days later, the funeral of Martin Petrovitch took place. The cost of the ceremony was undertaken by my mother, who was deeply grieved at his death, and gave orders that no expense was to be spared. She did not herself go to the church, because she was unwilling, as she said, to set eyes on those two vile hussies and that nasty little Jew. But she sent Kvitsinsky, me, and Zhitkov, though from that time forward she always spoke of the latter as a regular old woman. Souvenir she did not admit to her presence, and was furious with him for long after, saying that he was the murderer of her friend. He felt his disgrace acutely; he was continually running, on tiptoe, up and down the room, next to the one where my mother was; he gave himself up to a sort of scared and abject melancholy, shuddering and muttering, 'd'rectly!'

In church, and during the procession, Sletkin struck me as having recovered his self-possession. He gave directions and bustled about in his old way, and kept a greedy look-out that not a superfluous farthing should be spent, though his own pocket was not in question. Maximka, in a new Cossack dress, also a present from my mother, gave vent to such tenor notes in the choir, that certainly no one could have any doubts as to the sincerity of his devotion to the deceased. Both the sisters were duly attired in mourning, but they seemed more stupefied than grieved, especially Evlampia. Anna wore a meek, Lenten air, but made no attempt to weep, and was continually passing her handsome, thin hand over her hair and cheek. Evlampia seemed deep in thought all the time. The universal, unbending alienation, condemnation, which I had noticed on the day of Harlov's death, I detected now too on the faces of all the people in the church, in their actions and their glances, but still more grave and, as it were, impersonal. It seemed as though all those people felt that the sin into which the Harlov family had fallen—this great sin—had gone now before the presence of the one righteous Judge, and that for that reason, there was no need now for them to trouble themselves and be indignant. They prayed devoutly for the soul of the dead man, whom in life they had not specially liked, whom they had feared indeed. Very abruptly had death overtaken him.

'And it's not as though he had been drinking heavily, brother,' said one peasant to another, in the porch.

'Nay, without drink he was drunken indeed,' responded the other.

'He was cruelly wronged,' the first peasant repeated the phrase that summed it up.

'Cruelly wronged,' the others murmured after him.

'The deceased was a hard master to you, wasn't he?' I asked a peasant, whom I recognised as one of Harlov's serfs.

'He was a master, certainly,' answered the peasant, 'but still... he was cruelly wronged!'

'Cruelly wronged....' I heard again in the crowd.

At the grave, too, Evlampia stood, as it were, lost. Thoughts were torturing her... bitter thoughts. I noticed that Sletkin, who several times addressed some remark to her, she treated as she had once treated Zhitkov, and worse still.

Some days later, there was a rumour all over our neighbourhood, that Evlampia Martinovna had left the home of her fathers for ever, leaving all the property that came to her to her sister and brother-in-law, and only taking some hundreds of roubles.... 'So Anna's bought her out, it seems!' remarked my mother; 'but you and I, certainly,' she added, addressing Zhitkov, with whom she was playing picquet—he took Souvenir's place, 'are not skilful hands!' Zhitkov looked dejectedly at his mighty palms.... 'Hands like that! Not skilful!' he seemed to be saying to himself....

Soon after, my mother and I went to live in Moscow, and many years passed before it was my lot to behold Martin Petrovitch's daughters again.

XXX

But I did see them again. Anna Martinovna I came across in the most ordinary way.

After my mother's death I paid a visit to our village, where I had not been for over fifteen years, and there I received an invitation from the mediator (at that time the process of settling the boundaries between the peasants and their former owners was taking place over the whole of Russia with a slowness not yet forgotten) to a meeting of the other landowners of our neighbourhood, to be held on the estate of the widow Anna Sletkin. The news that my mother's 'nasty little Jew,' with the prune-coloured eyes, no longer existed in this world, caused me, I confess, no regret whatever. But it was interesting to get a glimpse of his widow. She had the reputation in the neighbourhood of a first-rate manager. And so it proved; her estate and homestead and the house itself (I could not help glancing at the roof; it was an iron one) all turned out to be in excellent order; everything was neat, clean, tidied-up, where needful—painted, as though its mistress were a German. Anna Martinovna herself, of course, looked older. But the peculiar, cold, and, as it were, wicked charm which had once so fascinated me had not altogether left her. She was dressed in rustic fashion, but elegantly. She received us, not cordially—that word was not applicable to her—but courteously, and on seeing me, a witness of that fearful scene, not an eyelash quivered. She made not the slightest reference to my mother, nor her father, nor her sister, nor her husband.

She had two daughters, both very pretty, slim young things, with charming little faces and a bright and friendly expression in their black eyes. There was a son, too, a little like his father, but still a boy to be proud of!

During the discussions between the landowners, Anna Martinovna's attitude was composed and dignified, she showed no sign of being specially obstinate, nor specially grasping. But none had a truer perception of their own interests than she of hers; none could more convincingly expound and defend their rights. All the laws 'pertinent to the case,' even the Minister's circulars, she had thoroughly mastered. She spoke little, and in a quiet voice, but every word she uttered was to the point. It ended in our all signifying our agreement to all her demands, and making concessions, which we could only marvel at ourselves. On our way home, some of the worthy landowners even used harsh words of themselves; they all hummed and hawed, and shook their heads.

'Ah, she's got brains that woman!' said one.

'A tricky baggage!' put in another less delicate proprietor. 'Smooth in word, but cruel in deed!'

'And a screw into the bargain!' added a third; 'not a glass of vodka nor a morsel of caviare for us—what do you think of that?'

'What can one expect of her?' suddenly croaked a gentleman who had been silent till then, 'every one knows she poisoned her husband!'

To my astonishment, nobody thought fit to controvert this awful and certainly unfounded charge! I was the more surprised at this, as, in spite of the slighting expressions I have reported, all of them felt respect for Anna Martinovna, not excluding the indelicate landowner. As for the mediator, he waxed positively eloquent.

'Put her on a throne,' he exclaimed, 'she'd be another Semiramis or Catherine the Second! The discipline among her peasants is a perfect model.... The education of her children is model! What a head! What brains!'

Without going into the question of Semiramis and

Catherine, there was no doubt Anna Martinovna was living a very happy life. Ease, inward and external, the pleasant serenity of spiritual health, seemed the very atmosphere about herself, her family, all her surroundings. How far she had deserved such happiness... that is another question. Such questions, though, are only propounded in youth. Everything in the world, good and bad, comes to man, not through his deserts, but in consequence of some as yet unknown but logical laws which I will not take upon myself to indicate, though I sometimes fancy I have a dim perception of them.

XXXI

I questioned the mediator about Evlampia Martinovna, and learnt that she had been lost sight of completely ever since she left home, and probably 'had departed this life long ago.'

So our worthy mediator expressed himself... but I am convinced that I *have seen* Evlampia, that I have come across her. This was how it was.

Four years after my interview with Anna Martinovna, I was spending the summer at Murino, a little hamlet near Petersburg, a well-known resort of summer visitors of the middle class. The shooting was pretty decent about Murino at that time, and I used to go out with my gun almost every day. I had a companion on my expeditions, a man of the tradesman class, called Vikulov, a very sensible and good-natured fellow; but, as he said of himself, of no position whatever. This man had been simply everywhere, and everything! Nothing could astonish him, he knew everything—but he cared for nothing but shooting and wine. Well, one day we were on our way home to Murino, and we chanced to pass a solitary house, standing at the cross-roads, and enclosed by a high, close paling. It was not the first time I had seen the house, and every time it excited my curiosity. There was something about it mysterious, locked-up, grimly-dumb, something suggestive of a prison or a hospital. Nothing of it could be seen from the road but its steep, dark, red-painted roof. There was only one pair of gates in the whole fence; and these seemed fastened and never opened. No sound came from the other side of them. For all that, we felt that some one was certainly living in the house; it had not at all the air of a deserted dwelling. On the contrary, everything about it was stout, and tight, and strong, as if it would stand a siege!

'What is that fortress?' I asked my companion. 'Don't you know?'

Vikulov gave a sly wink. 'A fine building, eh? The police-captain of these parts gets a nice little income out of it!'

'How's that?'

'I'll tell you. You've heard, I daresay, of the Flagellant dissenters—that do without priests, you know?'

'Yes.'

'Well, it's there that their chief mother lives.'

'A woman?'

'Yes—the mother; a mother of God, they say.'

'Nonsense!'

'I tell you, it is so. She is a strict one, they say.... A regular commander-in-chief! She rules over thousands! I'd take her, and all these mothers of God.... But what's the use of talking?'

He called his Pegashka, a marvellous dog, with an excellent scent, but with no notion of setting. Vikulov was obliged to tie her hind paws to keep her from running so furiously.

His words sank into my memory. I sometimes went out of my way to pass by the mysterious house. One day I had just got up to it, when suddenly—wonderful to relate!—a bolt grated in the gates, a key creaked in the lock, then the gates themselves slowly parted, there appeared a large horse's head, with a plaited forelock under a decorated yoke, and slowly there rolled into the road a small cart, like those driven by horse-dealers, and higglers. On the leather cushion of the cart, near to me, sat a peasant of about thirty, of a remarkably handsome and attractive appearance, in a neat black smock, and a black cap, pulled down low on his forehead. He was carefully driving the well-fed horse, whose sides were as broad as a stove. Beside the peasant, on the far side of the cart, sat a tall woman, as straight as an arrow. Her head was covered by a costly-looking black shawl. She was dressed in a short jerkin of dove-coloured velvet, and a dark blue merino skirt; her white hands she held discreetly clasped on her bosom. The cart turned on the road to the left, and brought the woman within two paces of me; she turned her head a little, and I recognised Evlampia Harlov. I knew her at once, I did not doubt for one instant, and indeed no doubt was possible; eyes like hers, and above all that cut of the lips—haughty and sensual—I had never seen in any one else. Her face had grown longer and thinner, the skin was darker, here and there lines could be discerned; but, above all, the expression of the face was changed! It is difficult to do justice in words to the self-confidence, the sternness, the pride it had gained! Not simply the serenity of power—the satiety of power was visible in every feature. The careless glance she cast at me told of long years of habitually meeting nothing but reverent, unquestioning obedience. That woman clearly lived surrounded, not by worshippers, but by slaves. She had clearly forgotten even the time when any command, any desire of hers, was not carried out at the instant! I called her loudly by her name and her father's; she gave a faint start, looked at me a second time, not with alarm, but with contemptuous wrath, as though asking—'Who dares to disturb me?' and barely parting her lips, uttered a word of command. The peasant sitting beside her started forward, with a wave of his arm struck the horse with the reins—the horse set off at a strong rapid trot, and the cart disappeared.

Since then I have not seen Evlampia again. In what way Martin Petrovitch's daughter came to be a Holy Virgin in the Flagellant sect I cannot imagine. But, who knows, very likely she has founded a sect which will be called—or even now is called—after her name, the Evlampieshtchin sect? Anything may be, anything may come to pass.

And so this is what I had to tell you of my *Lear of the Steppes*, of his family and his doings.

The story-teller ceased, and we talked a little longer, and then parted, each to his home.

Weimar, 1870.

CPSIA information can be obtained
at www.ICGtesting.com
Printed in the USA
FSHW04n0426050418
46314FS